DO YOU
FOLLOW?

J.C. BIDONDE

DO YOU
FOLLOW?

GREENLEAF
BOOK GROUP PRESS

Published by Greenleaf Book Group Press
Austin, Texas
www.gbgpress.com

Distributed by Greenleaf Book Group

For ordering information or special discounts for bulk purchases, please contact Greenleaf Book Group at PO Box 91869, Austin, TX 78709, 512.891.6100.

Design and composition by Greenleaf Book Group
Cover design by Greenleaf Book Group
Cover Image: ©iStockphoto/Savushkin, ©iStockphoto/The7Dew

Publisher's Cataloging-in-Publication data is available.

Print ISBN: 978-1-62634-902-5

eBook ISBN: 978-1-62634-903-2

Part of the Tree Neutral® program, which offsets the number of trees consumed in the production and printing of this book by taking proactive steps, such as planting trees in direct proportion to the number of trees used: www.treeneutral.com

TreeNeutral

Printed in the United States of America on acid-free paper

21 22 23 24 25 26 27   10 9 8 7 6 5 4 3 2 1

First Edition

To the mad ones, may you never stop burning.

1

ALEXA

September 17, 2021
NYC

The police station is just as I've always imagined—or rather, the same as I've seen in countless episodes of *Law & Order*. There is a large open area at the center, housing several clunky desks adorned with actual landline phones and computers. Veering off from the large room, like gates at an airport terminal, are an excessive number of rooms hidden by white aluminum blinds. Sounds are equally excessive—phones ringing, voices shouting, doors opening and closing. And the walls are pale green, of all colors.

I've always liked true crime television, but my experience today may change that. I understand they need to corral the alleged criminals, but what about those of us who are innocent? Shouldn't we get a fabric chair or something? Instead, I've been sitting in this cold, dingy interrogation room for hours. The office with the ratty blinds is starting to seem downright appealing. Hindsight and all that, I suppose.

One thing, though: This room doesn't have a two-way mirror—the kind that the lead detective always stands hidden behind, with a look of equal parts frustration and determination as he studies the tight-lipped criminal.

It's probably for the best that there is no mirror. I'm afraid of who I'd see in one.

I pass the time by fumbling with the now-empty Dixie cup, water being the only creature comfort they've given me since my arrival. Despite the mirror's absence, I know they're watching me—the cops are always watching these rooms. I don't know how I'm supposed to act. I'm not telling them that I had nothing to do with what happened, because that's not true. But I didn't kill him.

She did.

The only way to get out of this is by proving my innocence. But I have no idea how I'm going to do that without *her*. Beth, my twin sister. We've always been close, closer than most twins even. Every time I've needed her, she shows up. But something tells me that this time, it's different.

The doors in this place are heavy, so I hear the detective coming before I see him. He's alone this time, and I'm glad it's him and not the one with the mustache. The ones with thick mustaches always have something to prove, it seems. The soft lines around his brown eyes make him appear kinder—and I need kinder right now.

"Need a refill?" he asks.

I look down at the empty Dixie cup—I knew they were watching. As I tell him no, I scan the room for the hidden cameras. Nothing that I can detect.

"Okay then. Officer Morton will be back in a little while, but I figured we could keep talking. Are you ready?" he asks with what might be compassion, might be boredom.

"Sure," I reply.

"Ms. Martin, can you tell me what happened when you entered your apartment earlier this evening?" he starts, and I realize it was neither compassion nor boredom—it's the same tone you hear when speaking to a customer service representative who cannot communicate with you outside of their script.

"As I told you, I saw my boyfriend, Curt, lying in a pool of blood." I jump ahead, already off-script. "But I wasn't the one who killed him."

The memory of it makes me tremble and sends an actual shiver right up my spine. Curt, with his legs and arms splayed in different directions, his chest full of bullet holes. He didn't look human, probably because he wasn't anymore. His mouth was agape and his eyes wide open—he looked like a prop from a costume store. Not my boyfriend, not anymore. I look down and notice my hands are bright pink from being wrung together.

"Then who did?" he counters, startling me. He's managed to improvise—skipping the part where he forces me to tell him what happened again. How refreshing.

"Beth," I say for what feels like the fifteenth time. On *Law & Order*, once the suspect's alibi checks out, they let them go. But then I remember this one episode where the cops wanted it to be the guy on camera so badly that, even though he'd ratted the real killer out, the detectives just started the line of questioning all over again.

"Okay, Ms. Martin, let's start from the beginning again," he says, and that's when I realize they want it to be me, not Beth.

But why? I wonder as a thick fog blankets my brain, silencing the officer's words. Instead, I play back these last few months with Beth. She never liked Curt, but no matter how dark our sisterhood was, I never thought she'd do this.

Where did you go, Beth? You have to come back. I try to connect to her, but that feeling of connection is gone.

Like a cord cut, just a limp rope in my hand.

2

ALEXA

Three Months Earlier

Living at home means eating dinner at the ungodly hour of five o'clock. As Dad and I sit in awkward silence, I steal glances at his plate. He hasn't touched my latest Instagram recipe.

"Is it chicken?" he asks.

"Cauliflower, Dad," I manage with restraint. "I told you—it's a way to make veggies taste better so you can cut out fatty foods. Like chicken wings and fries."

Without looking up, he stabs one of the cauliflower florets with his fork and tosses the vegetable in his mouth. I can tell he's confused. The flavor from the Frank's RedHot sauce does say buffalo wings, but the texture is unmistakably vegetable. He chews the floret a lot longer than he would spend gnawing on a chicken wing.

"So?" I inquire hopefully.

"It tastes like cauliflower with hot sauce," he states.

"Yeah, I guess there's a little aftertaste," I say, steadying myself for the now-familiar monologue. After Mom passed away a few years ago, we survived on six-dollar drive-thru meals. Around my sophomore year of high school, I couldn't take it anymore and started cooking. I began with easy things like microwave veggies and boxed rice, and as I experimented, I got better. But he still prefers the artery-cloggers from the chain restaurants. We've compromised on breakfast and dinner—now eating those meals at home—but I can't control lunch.

"Well, if you're going to put the same hot sauce on vegetables, why not just have wings and eat the carrots and celery they give you? Chicken's good for you," he says, and, honestly, he has a point there. I'm preparing to go through the health benefits of cauliflower once more when my cell phone rings from the kitchen counter.

A 212 area code. Dr. Greer? No, I have his number saved. Maybe someone else from the Weinstein Center.

"Hello?" I say, picking up. I steal a glance at Dad. He's moved on to the kale salad, lifting a couple of small leafy pieces as if he's searching for something more appetizing beneath. I think I may have gone too far with tonight's dinner.

"Hey, Alexa!" an overly cheerful voice greets me. "It's Christine from FLLW."

"Oh! Yes, hi, Christine. How are you?" My voice has gone up three octaves to match hers, and Dad has taken the distraction as an opportunity to completely give up on dinner. He's set his fork down and is now watching with eager fatherly eyes.

"Good, good. Listen, everyone here just loved you. We'd love to have you join the team as a marketing assistant."

"Oh, my goodness. Wow. Thank you!"

I interviewed almost two weeks ago at FLLW, pronounced "follow." Since their main office is in Manhattan, it took me almost six months to convince Dad to let me interview. Dad wouldn't even let me go away to college; instead, I received my associate's in communication from Middlesex Community. That's the thing that surprises me the most about Christine's news; they don't care that I'm missing a bachelor's.

"The only catch is we needed someone, like, yesterday. So would you be able to start on the fifteenth?" she asks.

"Next week?" I say, walking to the kitchen as I do the math in my head.

"Yes. Can you do it?"

"Yeah, I think that would be fine. I mean, it's not that far, even if I don't have a place by then."

"Oh, totally! Plus, you know New York—when you find a place, you take it that minute," she says. Except I don't know New York. Not like that. I visit Dr. Greer every week, but Dad takes me, and the longest we stay is for a slice of pizza before heading back to Connecticut.

"That sounds about right," I say, keeping my voice neutral and upbeat. But already I can feel my heart pounding in my chest. *Excitement*, I tell myself. *Not fear.*

"I'll go ahead and email you all the details and salary information, okay, girl?" she says.

"Sounds great!" I chirp, although honestly, it's my first job; the fact I'll be paid anything is exciting enough. "I'm excited to be a part of the team." It's said with what I think may be too much enthusiasm, especially given Christine's cool and confident New Yorker demeanor. But I can't help it—I can't remember the last time I felt *happy* like this.

"Awesome. KK, talk soon!" she says.

"Okay, thank you! Bye," I say, although I'm fairly certain she's already hung up.

As I hit the end button, I turn around and am surprised to see that Dad has followed me into the kitchen. He's the loving-and-supportive-but-still-not-sure-how-to-handle-daughters kind of dad. Since Mom passed, he's slipped into a familiar shell.

"Did you get it?" he asks with cautious enthusiasm.

"Yeah," I say, the full reality of the call washing over me. "I got it!"

He reaches out to hug me. His hugs are still frequent, but there's an air of hesitation now, a trepidation not unlike how he approached the buffalo cauliflower. I'm his daughter, but he still misses Mom. And Beth. I'm the only one of us still here, and I'm not sure I'm his first choice. I think I used to be, but so much has changed.

"When do you start?" he asks when he pulls away.

"That's the thing," I begin as we return to the dining room. "They want me to start Monday."

"This Monday?"

"Yep."

"Oh, wow, that's quick. How do they expect you to have a place in the city by then?" he says, running his hands through his espresso-colored hair, the way he does when he's uncomfortable. I've seen it a lot. Finally, he sets them on either side of his plate, where almost every piece of the cauliflower remains.

"I'm not sure, but I think I should head in tomorrow and start looking."

He gives me a long stare. "Oh, Lex, I don't know. Are you sure you're ready?"

"We've talked about this. I've been doing so well with Dr. Greer. Plus, I'll be able to see him more frequently if I live in the city," I argue. This point was always my ace.

"I know," he says, then pauses. He looks at his plate, then back at me, and I can see the white flag rising. "I just worry about you, Lex—and I still worry about Beth."

And there it is, he's said it. The name that kicks us both out of the present moment. It registers in the faraway look in his eyes. I'm never sure where he goes, but I imagine it's to a time when Beth and I were little, or maybe to Mom. But for me, I go to the same place every time: the night it all changed, the night that Dad had finally had enough and sent Beth away. Dr. Greer wants to explore my reluctance to move on, but I don't want to leave it behind. In an odd way, it's comforting knowing there are some things that will never change.

I haven't told him that. I don't think I will.

My dad's fumbling with his beer bottle now, swirling it as if it's a fine wine, occasionally lifting it to peer through the small hole. There's nothing in there except beer, which can be very interesting, but I can see he's just trying to avoid an argument. I begged him not to kick her out. I pleaded for him to let her stay. I tried every combination of words under the sun in my attempts to make him understand, but he just stared at me as if I were speaking Mandarin. It was maddening. Until, finally, I gave up. When he says he worries about her, I don't think it's like a normal parent would. He doesn't worry for her safety. That's something I had to accept a while ago too.

Still, when I play by his rules and avoid Beth, he gives me more freedom. So, in some twisted way, he's won. I think about her every day, but we no longer speak.

I've spent most of my days missing her, but this time, I'm relieved that she isn't here. I know how she'd react to this new development in my life. She'd squish my excitement like a roach under a heavy work boot, barely noticing the destruction in her wake.

3

BETH

I've never understood why mental facilities always look like something right out of the pages of *Elle Décor* magazine. Every time I enter this lobby, with its obnoxious palm-frond wallpaper, oversized leather sofas, golden wall sconces, and perfectly herringboned tiled floors, I'm immediately nauseous. This is a goddamn looney bin— most of the patients don't even know their own name, let alone care about the aesthetics of their surroundings. Plus, isn't it a little counterproductive to give such a beautiful building to people with such little hope? Or perhaps the hope is only for their families, desperate to have in their view something that deflects the terror and hopelessness that they feel.

Today the reception desk is manned by the blonde receptionist with the offensive fingernails. They're filed to such a sharp point that I don't know how she wipes. She's usually looking down, texting under the desk, but today, in a shocking twist, she's on the landline. I think she's actually working.

Dr. Greer's office is down this long maze of a hallway. Unlike the lobby, the hallways are all decorated in the same style, with big black-and-white tiles that alternate like that of a chessboard. It's very distracting, as are the black-and-white photos lining the walls. I can't help but wonder if they ran short on budget after the lobby or if they hired the same interior designer as Kris Jenner. Either way, if I were crazy, these hallways would make it worse.

As I pass the rooms, I can't help but think of Alexa. I've never understood why she comes here willingly (I don't have a choice in the matter). Since the incident, Lex still seems pretty convinced there's something wrong with her. Something to fix. I've tried to explain that there's absolutely nothing wrong, but she's always been the naïve one, open to what everyone suggests is the reality rather than relying on her own mental processes.

The black-and-white photos are just repeating depictions of elephants, giraffes, lions, and zebras, the silver grassy backdrop behind them seeming to glow under the African sun. I make a silent vow to never look at them—between the tiles, the photos, and the zebras, I'm going to lose it myself. Maybe that's why they chose the décor, to ensure repeat customers. The revelation makes me laugh.

I make a turn, but as I reach the end of this second hallway, I realize I must have taken a wrong turn. To my right is a pair of double doors leading to a large room, and to my left, the bathrooms. I haven't been down this hallway before.

I enter the large room. Twenty round wooden tables, each surrounded by eight matching black chairs, sit empty. There are apples, bananas, a coffee machine, and a basket of KIND bars. I smile as I grab an apple. They really had to go with the KIND brand granola bars—RX bars wouldn't be appropriate. Clif would be simply wrong.

I head back to the checkered halls to continue looking for Alexa, but I'm stopped when a white blur slams into me from one side.

"Fuck! Sorry, didn't see you there," says a raspy male voice. When my brain catches up, I recognize that the speaker is a tall blond man with an apron hugging his athletic physique. He's setting down his metal tray of assorted baked goods, and as he does, three croissants fall to the floor. I only get a good look at his face when he brings the fallen pastries to his mouth and blows whatever invisible germs may have gotten on them during their affair with the floor.

I'm not a huge germaphobe—in fact, Howie Mandel annoys me. Not because he's a germaphobe but because he was so ahead of his time. Who knew he was right all these years? A true social-distancing pioneer. That's what bugs me.

I notice that Apron Guy is staring at me, almost as if he knows what I'm thinking. Fuck.

"No worries," I reply, turning on my heel and trying to hide my disgust at his adoption of the five-second rule.

"Hey!" he calls after me.

I turn back, a massive bite from my apple pushed to the left side of my mouth.

"How are you doing?" he says, an odd expression in his green eyes.

"Pretty good, thanks." I can't help but feel bad for this weirdo. They clearly let the patients work in the kitchen here, like those weeks in elementary school where they forced students to prep and serve tray lunches. I always hated that one week a year when it was my turn to don the hairnet and serve my peers. We all had to do it, but it always sucked when it was your turn. It was almost as bad as when it was the kid who always used his sleeve to wipe his perpetually running nose.

"Good!" he says, still staring at me.

"Okay, cool." I hoist up the apple in a gesture meant to signify both "thank you" and "we're done here." He seems to understand, so I turn and head for the double doors.

"See you later!" he shouts, then thankfully leaves me alone when someone calls out for him to drop the tray and help chop onions for lunch.

As I wander down four or five more hallways, my frustration grows. The hunt for Dr. Greer's office makes me miss the old days, when I'd wander the halls of our elementary school to find Alexa. Until fourth grade, the school never had any issue with us being in the same class. But I'd seen them separate the Johnson twins in first grade, so I suppose, on some level, I knew it was coming. When we got the notice that she was in Mr. Gleeson's class, we were all shocked to see I'd been assigned to Mrs. Hobbs. I developed a little ploy early in the year. I'd sneak out under the pretext of a bathroom break and go peek into Alexa's classroom.

It's not that I couldn't handle being separated, but Alexa is unknowing, gullible, and at times downright weak. When I heard a rumor that she was being picked on, I had to make sure she was okay—just like any good sister. The first time she saw me spying on her through the slim rectangular window, her face was priceless. She was so excited she stood up at her desk and waved at me, narrowly missing the consternation of her teacher, who was distracted with scrawling numbers on the chalkboard.

I'm at the end of another goddamn hallway when I spot another restroom, a welcome opportunity for a break. To my delight, the restroom is the color of a California poppy, and the four stall doors are each adorned with gold handles and a round circle lock. I can tell someone is in the far one from the sound of the flush.

I don't have to use the restroom, so I stand at the sink, waving my hands in front of the faucet sensor. It spits water intermittently as I wash the apple juice from my hands. I stare at my thick dark brown hair in the mirror. I've always loved it. While we were different in so many ways, Alexa and I both liked to keep our hair long, wearing it down and letting it fall like a security blanket around our faces.

The stall door opens, and I hear feet approaching the sink.

"Ms. Miller?"

It's Patricia, Dr. Greer's nurse practitioner.

"Oh. Hi, Patricia," I reply with little enthusiasm.

"You're late," she states flatly as she motions for the touchless faucet to begin.

"When duty calls."

She forces a smile, and I stifle my desire to say something snarky. As she waves her hands, now under the paper towel dispenser, I take a final look in the mirror and steel myself to follow her to my session.

I follow her mousy ash-brown bob through the maze of black-and-white halls until we finally reach his door. Patty opens the door for me, and I step through, only catching her gaze for long enough to see the tiny crooked scar above her left eyebrow, marring her otherwise perfectly smooth forehead. I never noticed it before. I suppose I never really looked at her much, but today I see it and it bothers me. I hate scars—they always serve as this dark reminder that you can't go back in time, that some things are forever and you can't change them.

"Ah, Ms. Miller, good to see you," Dr. Greer greets me.

"Hi, sorry. Train traffic," I reply.

"Well, it's your time, as you know."

Dad, or Dad's insurance, pays Dr. Greer. So even when I'm absent or late—and I'm absent a lot these days—he's always compensated. Dr. Greer has explained this to me several times throughout the years of therapy.

I settle into one of the office's two large tobacco-colored leather chairs. He rarely stands to greet me anymore. We're like an old married couple, a little too comfortable—or maybe it's complacent. Either way, Dr. Greer knows us, our story, and our family. We've seen him for most of our lives. On most days, I'm quiet.

"How have you been?" he begins.

"Fine." The words leave my mouth too quickly. From Dr. Greer's expression, I can tell he knows I'm lying. I have to give the man credit—he knows when there's more to my story. And today, there is. I feel like talking.

"I think I'm pretending to be okay. But I don't really feel okay," I tell him.

His face barely moves at this admission. He's unfazed.

"There have been so many changes," I continue.

"For you?" he asks.

"Yes. And for my sister," I say.

"Have you spoken to her recently?"

"No."

He looks at me as if searching for the truth somewhere below the surface of my skin. He seems to be placated.

"How do you feel about that?" he asks.

"I miss her."

"She likely misses you as well."

"I doubt it." I think back to the emails of hers I've read. Figuring out her password was easy. At the treatment center Dad sentenced me to a year ago, we were allowed only an hour a day

to use the internet, but I was able to crack it on the first day—
BIEBERWIFE. Twins can't keep secrets from each other, but she
also hasn't changed it since we were little. Her obsession with Justin
Bieber transitioned a little too easily through each stage of adoles-
cence. I never really got the appeal of him, but he has had a few
bangers that I can't deny.

"As we've worked on, you are two separate beings. Yes, you're
twins, but it would be impossible to really know what she's thinking
and feeling," he reminds me. "Then, or now, if she was able to be
in the room with us for this session."

But I know she doesn't miss me. She's elated to be on her own,
with a new job, in a new city. When I finally left the facility a few
months ago, I was released to a transitional home for women where
I had more internet time to keep close tabs on her inbox. I knew
she'd move on, likely start her adult life, but seeing the job offer was
excruciating. I immediately asked for a transfer from the glorified
halfway house up north to one in White Plains, but somehow, just
last week, they agreed to release me instead.

"Can you tell me more about why you feel like you're pretending to be okay?" he asks.

"No."

"Why not?"

"Because I don't know. I just feel . . ." I trail off, searching for
the word.

"Disconnected."

"Yeah, I guess."

"From her?"

"From everything."

He nods, but I see a frustration wash over him. Generalities are
not what therapists want to hear. They want the nitty-gritty details

of our brains' inner workings. So our little dialogue has taken a sharp right turn toward unproductive. To my surprise, I'm disappointed too. I don't dislike Dr. Greer. And, on occasion, I do open up. I thought today would be one of those days. He did too. But now here we are, at a standstill.

"Want to tell me about how you think all of your time here has gone?" he asks. "How you feel about our work together?"

I shake my head, and he turns toward the TV hanging in the corner. It's the only other thing we can do to finish the session with a semblance of productivity. I have never felt particularly warm toward Dr. Greer. He's never done anything outwardly awful or wrong, but I just don't want him in my business. Our business. After this many years, what else does he possibly have to wonder about me?

"Brené Brown it is," he chirps as he goes to play yet another clip from the shame expert.

"I don't feel ashamed."

He quickly shuts down my attempt to avoid Brené. "We all have shame. You know this."

"If I watch this, will you discharge me?"

"You know your discharge is today. This is simply to wrap up inpatient treatment and to get a sense of where you are at as we start you on intensive outpatient work."

"Well, can we skip the video?" I try with a cheeky smile I rarely give.

"Humor me, will you?"

I take a deep breath and settle into the chair. Its worn-in softness welcomes me but hardly hugs me.

4

ALEXA

The East Coast is known for its traditions, architecture, and stereotypically aggressive inhabitants, but I've always loved the thick foliage. Trees line the highways like the crowds at the Macy's Thanksgiving Day Parade, there to see Snoopy and friends coming down Madison Avenue.

I know how to drive, but Dad always insists. He's not a bad driver in Connecticut, but I worry once we reach the city, as the madness of cabs and pedestrians makes him nervous—even when we don't have stacks of boxes piled to the ceiling. Today our forest-green Jeep Grand Cherokee could be its own self-contained episode of *Hoarders*, despite the fact that movers handled most of the larger items. The additional blind spots would make maneuvering hard for a seasoned cabby, let alone my suburban-dwelling father.

As we round the last bend, the trees start to recede, and Dad's silence turns into chatter.

"Yeah, I don't know how people drive in this city."

"They don't," I say with a smile. "Well, the smart ones don't. That's why you have the almighty metro card." Instinctively, I reach for my wallet to check if I still have mine.

"Ah yes, the subway." He sighs. "You feel comfortable using that to get around?"

"Yes, Dad. They have these crazy things called apps"—I wave my phone in his peripheral vision—"and some genius invented one that not only routes you to your final destination but also lets you select your preferred mode of transportation. Even these outdated things are a legitimate option," I say, propping my feet on the dash and wiggling my toes.

"Okay, okay, I get it. You're all grown up," he says with a laugh. "Just know that if you need anything, I'm only an hour away—or five, with traffic."

"I know, Dad. And I have Dr. Greer close by if there's any emergency," I assure him. In fact, we were supposed to see him earlier today, stopping on our way to the apartment to do a quick talk about the transition, but Dad must have canceled the appointment, because he didn't say anything about it this morning as we were packing up the last odds and ends. I must have dozed off somewhere between White Plains and the city, because once I came to, we had long passed Dr. Greer's office and were nearing my block. Of course I wasn't going to say anything. One less thing to deal with today, which suits me just fine.

The trees have given way to the concrete jungle, but I can still see the Hudson River snaking along the West Side Highway—the last reminder of the serene hometown I've left behind. We finally turn away from it and onto Twenty-Third Street, at which point I glue my forehead to the window and watch the people and buildings. I'm always surprised by the amount of color. Neon signs, red-toned brick, iron fire escapes, and millions of different skin tones. The city looks like one of those blurred images a photographer captures, just streaks of colors in a completely still image. Life moving too quickly to capture. That's New York City.

We turn down Seventh Avenue, and I watch as tiny cobblestone side streets wander off the busy avenue. I've always loved the West Village. The few times Dad has let me come in to see Dr. Greer on my own, I've wandered downtown, blaming my late return on the omnipresent NYC traffic. Each downtown street seems to unfold in a new direction, making it impossible not to get lost, and I love it. Filled with people and noise at all hours, the New York streets provide me with the one thing a small town cannot: privacy. New York City is the one place I know where no one is really watching.

After a few turns and near misses with pedestrians, we arrive at Bedford Street, the site of the small walk-up apartment I found two days prior on StreetEasy. The virus has left nothing but a dark memory for most, but for me, it means a more affordable apartment in the West Village. Selfish, maybe, but it's the truth.

We find parking on an even narrower street that flanks the back of the building, a miraculous accomplishment even post-pandemic. I open the rear side door of the Jeep, and two pillows slump out. I pick them up, noticing the stains of the city street smeared across the clean white cases, then tuck them under my arm as Dad rounds the rear with one of the larger boxes.

"This way!" I nod, and he follows.

After fumbling with the keys that the agent messengered over the day before, we go through two sets of glass doors and then stop in the marble entry. This has to be the original flooring—once opulent, it now bears almost as many cracks as the pavement outside. The stairs in the building are old as well. As we head up to the third floor, I make a mental note on the second-floor landing not to wear heels or carry too many groceries home—the steps are surprisingly steep.

We find my door, the first to the left of the staircase. It was once a bright blue, but the years of wear have dulled it to a murky blue green. Two other doors of the same hue line the hall. Shifting my pillows, I manage to open the door to a welcoming beam of sunlight across the hardwood floors.

"Gosh, Lex. It's pretty small," Dad says from behind his bulky box. He's still trying to catch his breath.

We walk down the narrow hallway. The "walk-in" closet is to the right. Just past it, on the left, is the entrance to the "kitchen," although it has been designated as such in the loosest sense. Anywhere other than New York, a kitchen means a refrigerator, freezer, microwave, oven, stove, sink, and garbage disposal. Here, I have a refrigerator and a sink, sans garbage disposal, and a tiny oven with two electric burners as my stove. All of the other staple kitchen items seem to have been overlooked by whoever converted this old building.

Another interesting addition is the door just beyond the sink, which is one uneven step up. Through this secret passage is the bathroom, which contains the smallest tub I've ever seen, as if a normal tub just had a baby and that baby tub was taken and placed here in my new apartment, the cramped space forever stunting its growth.

The living room, which is also small, houses the furniture that came with the apartment. The walls somehow hug both sides of the sofa loosely enough that I think I'll be able to fit the floor lamp I brought from home. I have windows but not a lot of natural light. The espresso-colored wood coffee table sits too largely in the middle of the space and screams outdated. Thankfully, a TV is mounted on the wall, so there's enough space to pass to the small pocket door leading to the bedroom. There is only enough capacity for a double bed, tall slim dresser, and small night table for a lamp. The presence of one decent-sized window keeps the room cozy, not claustrophobic.

"You know New York—you lived here once," I remind him.

"Yeah, but that was the seventies. I'm fairly certain they spliced up my tiny apartment into eight new shoeboxes for you kids," he jokes. "Oh, and then multiplied the rent by eight."

"Times ten actually. But I'll take two hundred and forty-six square feet. It's my little safe haven in this mass of people."

After putting down his box, he stands with hands on his hips. "I suppose you're right. Moving to the city is a rite of passage."

"One I wasn't sure I was ever going to have."

I regret the words as soon as they leave my mouth. He gives me the look, but this time no words of caution come with it. Instead, he begins to drag the large box to the corner of the room, which doesn't take long, as it is about four steps for him to cross the room. I almost think I've dodged the consequences when he speaks.

"Have you heard from Beth lately?" he asks, his back still turned to me as he carefully aligns the box with the edges of the walls, so that it fits as snugly into the corner as possible.

"No," I assure him. It's the same answer I've given him for fourteen months now.

Finally satisfied with the arrangement of the box, he turns around and faces me. His eyes tell me he's still concerned, so I flash my most easygoing smile.

"Well, let's get the rest of them," he says, signaling that the Beth discussion is over, at least for now.

We retrace our steps over and over, moving my little life packed in boxes. When the last of my things are safely inside my apartment, Dad organizes them into stacks in the corner, saying he wants to free up as much space as possible for me to unpack later. He dusts off his hands, as if to signal a day's work coming to an end.

"Do you want to grab a bite before I have to head back?" he asks.

"Sure!"

"Slice?" he suggests, although he knows the answer.

"Salad?"

"Come on, Lex. I think it's actually against the law to leave Manhattan without a proper slice."

I can argue with Dad on almost anything, but he has a point on this one.

We arrive at Joe's after two short blocks. Since it's three o'clock in the afternoon on a Thursday, there's only one person in front of us. Joe's is famous in the city. Celebrities frequent the place, fully willing to stand with the rest of us in a line that normally wraps around the corner onto Sixth Avenue.

Inside, a young couple laughs beneath the rows of famous-people photos while playfully arguing over how best to eat their pieces of pizza. I watch as the woman dramatically flips her brown ponytail to the side and tilts her head, lowering the pointed end of her folded pepperoni slice into her mouth.

Her boyfriend watches with admiration and a wide smile before taking a bite of his unfolded cheese one. "See, if you leave it flat, there's more opportunity for bites. Don't you want the slice to last as long as possible?" I hear him argue.

"No!" she exclaims, then takes another massive bite.

Usually, I never order anything besides cheese. But when the round-faced Italian man at the counter asks what kind, I tell him, "Pepperoni." I want to be on the other end of that argument and the boyfriend's loving eyes. I've wondered for a while now what it would be like to be loved by a man. The truth is, I've never been the object of anyone's desire. I've blamed it on being from a small town, on being too nerdy, but it's most likely my family's drama that has kept the male sex at bay. But now, in this big city, no one knows me. And no one knows Beth.

5

ALEXA

Dad leaves shortly after we devour our slices of pizza. Instead of heading back to the apartment, I decide to walk around my new neighborhood, partly to explore but mostly to finally feel what it's like to walk the city streets without preparing excuses for why I'm late coming back to Connecticut. For the first time in my life, I report to no one.

I'm truly alone.

Growing up with a twin sister had its perks, but there were challenges too. I remember how lucky I felt that I had a built-in ally and playmate. They say twins share a unique connection, but ours was truly remarkable. We always knew what the other was thinking. I'm not sure how, but our ability to communicate without words still exists. I never imagined we'd be living such separate lives. I think for Beth, it all changed after the incident. But for me, it was our mother's death. That was the moment I saw life—and my sister—a little differently.

I get so lost thinking about her that I don't even know how my new neighborhood creeps up on me so quickly, but there it is. I pass the last of the multimillion-dollar brownstones that pave the way to my more modest building. As I look at them, perfectly manicured, I think of Carrie Bradshaw from *Sex and the City*—there's no way she lived in that brownstone on her salary and spending habits. Mine is expensive enough, and it's the size of her bathroom.

Once inside, I decide to begin unpacking the boxes containing my clothes because they are the simplest to organize. The walk-in closet is as advertised. You can walk into it. However, you cannot dress or undress in it without knocking all the hanging items on either side to the floor. I start in the back, which is only three feet from the front, and hang up the blouses I've acquired for my new job.

I move on to the kitchen next. Dad was kind enough to send me with some extra sets of tableware. Mom had this weird habit of discount shopping for plates, glassware, and cutlery. We rarely had dinner guests, so I always assumed it was a hobby. Regardless, I tell myself she'd be happy they are getting some use. Dad is probably relieved to have one less reminder.

I'm loading the white plates with the shiny floral motif onto the bottom shelf when I hear my sister. I can't quite understand what she's saying, but I'd recognize her voice anywhere. I freeze as I strain to listen to her. Can it be? Is she really here, or am I hallucinating?

I walk quietly to the door, listening to what seems to be her side of a conversation. I look through the peephole and see her, clearly talking on her phone.

Shock courses through my body as I realize she's really here. I guess I didn't think that she'd come see me so soon. It's only been a few hours since Dad left . . . and I was still adjusting to being in this new space, all mine. Or at least it was. I reach for the locks and begin to disarm my door, ready to welcome my sister in.

6

BETH

After the therapy session is over, I head downtown. Why are people so obsessed with this city? I've been meandering my way to the subway for twenty minutes, and the whole time it's been like being a pinball inside a machine. As another stranger grazes my left arm, I try to jerk to the right, but something sticky keeps my right foot from moving gracefully. I look down to find something unidentifiable on the bottom of my shoe. I try to subtly scrape the mess onto the subway floor, wondering how many millions of other people have done the same thing on these cesspools.

The subway rattles as it shimmies through the tunnels. I look around at my fellow miserable passengers, and I keep wondering why Alexa would pick this hellhole as the launchpad for her independence. The shrill of metal wheels grinding against metal tracks snaps me from my thoughts. When I see we're whizzing past the West Fourth Street sign, I feel a childlike euphoria knowing that my time on this filthy tin can is coming to an end.

The doors to the subway spring open, and the familiar stale and stinky heat smacks me like a boxing glove to the face. July in this city is the worst. We've come here all our lives, but the summer is intolerable. The heat somehow sinks down into the elaborate tunnel system and waits patiently to consume whoever dares enter.

I slip past what feels like thousands of people before I finally see the sunlight cascading down the steps—my final challenge before I'm freed from commuter hell.

I ascend the steps quickly, careful not to touch another person. A woman with a stroller struggles to hold her baby while attempting to maneuver the oversized contraption down the crowded stairwell. I look at her long enough for her to see me. When she does, her eyes search mine as if she's reading the CliffsNotes of my soul. She wants to know if I will help her. I do not. As her face drops, I recite my silent mantra: *You got what you deserve*. Women have babies for the most idiotic reasons. An excuse to buy cute clothes, the shower, the presents, the fucking Instagram photos. Well, serves you right that you can't function as a normal human being.

Everything has a price.

That's the one thing about the city that I like. There's so much struggle here. It's entertaining to watch. Every city block is its own episode of *Keeping Up with the Kardashians*, but it's real. No fourth wall.

When I emerge above ground, I have to pause for a second. New York City is largely on a grid, which means even the most moronic of humans can figure out how to get around without a map. But downtown gets messy—the streets crisscross and zigzag with no particular pattern in mind. Just a bunch of winding, suddenly ending or beginning streets to confuse the people on them into feeling as though they're in some magical place, when really they're just in a concrete puzzle. I figure it's because that's where the creatives live. And the addicts. There are endless creative souls down here, searching for inspiration in the next pill, sip, or puff. Just a bunch of imposters hoping a bottle of Wild Turkey will make them the next Hemingway. But who the fuck wants to be Hemingway—famous and successful, sure, but also depressed?

Probably a Kardashian. Duh.

I stroll the couple hundred yards down Sixth Avenue—past sex shops, smoke shops, and a few more elevated storefronts—before I see a gaggle of teenagers laughing and indulging in hot dogs at Gray's Papaya.

As I watch them laugh and eat, I wonder how this group came together. Likely through school. School was never my favorite place. I always felt like an outsider, invisible. Except to Alexa. She was supposed to be my built-in best friend.

As it does more often than not when I think of the incident, my hand instinctively lowers to my left flank.

Shaking it off, I stroll past the teenagers and round the corner. I'm only a couple of blocks from her new apartment. I still can't believe she did it. *Little Lex is all grown up*, I think to myself and smile. But just as fast, my smile falls.

Why couldn't she wait?

The scream of a fire engine howls so loudly that all thoughts are literally silenced while I plug my ears to quiet the wail. I come back to my surroundings just as I'm passing a pizza place. I think about stopping for a slice, but instead I keep my path and head for Alexa.

The entrance to her building proffers the obstacles of two sets of glass doors. I've never understood glass doors. They do little for privacy or protection. I turn to the antiquated box to the left of the first one. Names cascade down in two columns. Next to each name is a button. I place one finger on the top left column and one on the right. Then I slowly run my fingers down, hitting each button.

I wait, but no one buzzes me in. I wait a little longer.

I return my fingers to their starting position and begin again, this time pressing each button for several seconds. I'm only halfway down the list when I hear the buzzer. New Yorkers, so distrusting until it comes to their deliveries. There's a ninety-nine percent chance that, at any given moment of the day, at least one person in any building in the city is waiting for a delivery of some kind. They won't make eye contact on the street, but they'll buzz any riffraff into the building if they think it's their Sweetgreen order.

I pass through the second glass door, which, come to find out, doesn't even lock. I'll need to warn Alexa about that. As I pass through the tiny lobby, I stop only briefly to admire the building bulletin board. There's an ad for babysitting, some flyer for a shitty-looking band, and one for a man seeking a date with a nerdy woman. Really? I follow the page to the bottom, where someone has actually taken one of the pre-cut numbers. *No way*, I think and tear one off. Chuckling, I tuck it in my pocket and head up the stairs.

By the time I reach the third floor, I realize the weight of the situation. I haven't seen Alexa in over a year—her wish, not mine. After Dad kicked me out, Alexa still saw me for a bit, but it wasn't long before she grew distant. Maybe it was something Dad said, or maybe it was that damn Dr. Greer.

I'm suddenly unsure how to make my entrance. I'd planned on, well, knocking on the door. But now, as I'm standing here, it doesn't feel right. Instead, I reach into my back pocket for my cell phone.

"Oh my gosh, I know!" I exclaim. "Did you see what she was wearing? I literally cannot," I tell the other end of the line, loud enough for my sister to hear. I continue my *Gossip Girl*-esque phone call until I hear her steps behind the door. The peephole goes dark, and that's how I know she sees me. I keep twirling my hair and commiserating with the fake recipient of my call.

Finally, I hear the latches slowly unlock. First the slide of the chain, then what sounds like a deadbolt. Lastly, I see the final lock release as the knob twists, the door opening to reveal my reflection.

My sister. Alexa.

7

ALEXA

"Beth," I say with equal parts excitement and fear. "What are you doing here?" Before she has time to respond, I follow up with the most important question: "How did you know where I live?"

"No 'hey,' 'hi,' or 'how are you'?" she retorts in that arrogant tone I loathe yet is nonetheless impressive in its assertiveness. She leans in for a hug. "One year and your manners are shot to shit, huh?"

My arms lie still at my sides as my brain tries to comprehend what's happening. "Hi," I force out as she releases her embrace. "How are you?"

"Good, good, good. You know, just living the dream," she says as she saunters past me into my apartment.

I haven't seen her in over a year. She looks the same—or maybe I'm just so used to seeing my own reflection that my brain can't decipher the difference. The thought sends a shiver down my spine. Her brown hair falls loosely over her black leather jacket. She looks thinner in her signature torn jeans, but then again, we've always been on the more petite side—envious of the beautiful curves other women have.

Taking a deep breath, I ask her again why she's here. I've missed her, but I'd begun to accept our separation.

"Look, I was in town, and I'd heard through the grapevine that you'd just moved to the city."

A lie. There's no grapevine—Beth isn't in touch with anyone from home except me.

"Is it so wrong to want to see my sister?" she says.

I rub my eyes and adjust my neck, back and forth, until I hear the pop I wanted. Then I sigh. "It is good to see you, Beth."

I wait for her to continue, which I know she will. Beth has never felt comfortable with silence—saying or doing anything to fill the space. When we were little, Mom once jokingly accused Beth of verbal diarrhea and gave her a gentle lecture on letting others talk. It didn't go over well. In any case, Dr. Greer thinks it's her desire to be in control.

"Cute place, Lex. Love what you've done with it." She gestures to the empty boxes decorating the tiny living room.

"I moved in today, Beth. Dad left only a matter of hours ago—give me a minute to get settled before you bash my new apartment, please."

"Dad. How is the old man?" she asks, but I can tell she doesn't really care.

"He's good," I lie. He hasn't been "good" since we were nine, and he's been even less good since Mom—both things she knows. But I refuse to give her the satisfaction.

"Good. To. Hear."

She says it like one of the Instagram influencers at FLLW, who speak with a pause between words. I. Don't. Get. It.

"So . . . ," I start, searching once again for the motive behind my sister's visit. And how she found me on this particular day, in this brand-new apartment that I have barely set foot inside. And why she isn't at the hospital.

"I got released," she shares proudly.

I freeze, unable to quiet the scream inside my head.

"I hate that I've been gone for so long. I've missed you. I figured I could stay with you for a bit," she half asks. "Just until I figure out my own place."

I can't bring myself to say no, but I don't say yes.

"Come on, it will be so fun. Just like old times."

Her smile's so wide I don't trust it. Released?

But what if the old times were not always good, I say in my head.

"Like the good times," she adds, as if she's read my mind.

I take another deep breath, looking at my sister's face. Most twins have some kind of physical distinction. A vocal quirk, a freckle, a crooked tooth. Something to help others—or themselves—differentiate between the two. But Beth and I were born truly identical. It's rare. The thought softens me, and nostalgia begins to soften my heart.

"Does Dad know?" I ask.

"Fuck no!" she shouts. "We are adults, Alexa. And fuck Dad. He sent me there in the first place. Like I was some kind of loony. Jesus."

Her voice has a hysterical note I know well.

"Okay, I'm sorry," I soothe.

"You can't say anything, Alexa. He'll try to separate us!" she shouts, worry buzzing in every word.

"Fine. But you have to lie low," I say.

"Yasss!" she shouts, the jovial spirit returning to her voice at an alarming pace. "Should we get takeout? I'm starving."

"I just had a slice of pizza," I respond automatically. "But that was a couple of hours ago, and it was only one slice." Going against Beth is never a good idea, even when it comes to things as simple as eating.

"Thai?" she asks.

"Sure," I agree.

I pick up my cell phone and open my favorite delivery app. I didn't use them much until the pandemic, when Dad and I started to rely on takeout more than ever—groceries, dinner, coffee . . . everything really. I still use them pretty frequently, and given the size of my kitchen, I imagine I'll continue to be a pretty loyal customer.

Shit. The Thai places all have at least an hour wait. Let's hope she didn't have her heart set on it.

"Chinese okay?" I ask her.

"Yeah. Fine. I want lo mein and kung pao chicken. The usual," she says, followed by a wink and a shooting motion with her hand. She always used to do that. Her thumb shoots straight up, her index finger straight out, forming the ninety-degree angle, while the rest of her fingers fold into her palm. Her "hand gun," I'd call it. A joke just between us.

I smile. "Well, since you're here, you can finish helping me unpack while we wait."

She nods before squeezing past me, up the step and into the tiny lavatory. She's humming some kind of song as she appears to take a mental inventory of the unloaded towels, washrags, and other bathroom items. The now-empty box sits on the floor, competing for space with the infant tub and mini toilet. Beth stands there with her chin in her hand, her index finger tapping her cheek. The holes in her jeans look cute. I search my memory for what my body is currently feeling and finally admit to myself that it is good to see her. Despite her serious drama, I missed my sister. I always miss my sister when she disappears.

I'm breaking down boxes in the living room when I hear the buzzer sound. Before I can react, Beth shouts, "Food's here!" I shake off her superfluous remark and make my way around boxes to the call box. I press the buzzer for a few seconds, allowing the driver to enter the building.

He must have run up the stairs at breakneck speed, because it's only a matter of seconds before I hear his knock on the door, and I am still fighting with lock number three, which seems to stick. "Open sesame," Beth offers from the living room, and the door swings open. I exchange pleasantries with the young delivery driver, who's still wearing his bike helmet and an N95 mask as he hands me the food. *Does he have it?* I wonder. If so, he's clearly not symptomatic, the trek up the stairs having done nothing to wind him. I'm vaccinated, but it still unnerves me to see people wearing the masks, like a new strain is coming.

"Kung pao to start for you?" Beth asks once we've set up in the kitchen. She's holding out a white cardboard carton by the slim silver handle.

"Sure." I take the carton.

"Chopsticks," she says, handing some over.

"Switch in the middle?" I ask.

"Duh!"

Beth hops up onto the lone counter in my small kitchen. I lean my back against the doorframe and dig into the carton. After a couple of bites, the discomfort of the doorframe guides me to a seated position at its base. I sit "crisscross applesauce," as Mom used to call it, stealing looks at my sister between bites.

"Isn't it nuts?" she says to break the silence.

"Isn't what nuts?"

"That so much time can pass, but then it feels like none has passed?" she explains.

"Yeah," I say, but it's only because I don't know how else to respond without upsetting her. I don't mention that I actually had my heart set on Thai.

"Look." She waves her empty chopsticks back and forth between the two of us. "Here we are, a year without seeing each other, and yet we're sitting in the same positions we always have, eating the usual Chinese takeout order." After taking a bite, she adds, mouth still full, "Like nothing has changed at all."

I pause, making a show of chewing my food to buy myself time before I have to respond. Then I pop my neck again, crafting my response.

"Nothing has changed? I have my own apartment in New York City. I start my first job—a real job—on Monday," I explain.

"I mean between us," she retorts, jamming her chopsticks into her food and setting the carton down forcefully.

"*Beth*. So much has changed between us. *I've* changed."

She laughs. "You haven't changed, Lex," she says, as if it's a fact.

Even though it stings, I don't argue with her or defend my claim. Instead, I force a laugh and look down at my kung pao chicken. "Trade?" I ask.

"Sure."

I take the carton, then settle back into my doorframe seat, delighting in the sweetness of the dish. I hate spicy food. Beth knows I hate spicy food, but our entire life we've shared meals this way. She orders what she wants, and I never challenge her. It's easier to go with Beth's flow than to go against it. It wasn't always this way, but after the incident, there was a shift—like a knife cutting through the flesh of a ribeye steak, separating our life into two distinct parts: before and after. Beth tries to deny it, but it's as undeniable as an earthquake.

I begin to make my way through the lo mein. She didn't eat

very much. I look to Beth, who appears to be scraping the bottom of the kung pao chicken. I feel a tinge of guilt for overeating.

"I think I may head to bed," I tell her.

She sighs. "Ugh, you're so lame!"

"I know, but I need to get the rest of the apartment set up and prepare for Monday."

She hops off the counter and heads for the sofa, where I've left a neatly folded sheet and blanket for her, and the better of my two pillows. I collect the trash and toss it in the tiny bin below the sink. I stand and turn to join her, but she's right next to me in the tiny kitchen entryway. She's looking at me and reaches for my hands, and I let her take them. She pulls me into a hug. This time I move my arms around her waist.

"I've really missed you, Lex," she whispers in my ear.

"Me too," I respond. But in my mind, I can only focus on my right arm. I can't feel the scar beneath her white tee, but I know it's there. I think about it every day. Bile rises at the thought.

Forcing the bile back down, I release her, hoping she hasn't sensed anything weird, which is like hoping that the back of your hand won't look like the back of your hand.

She smiles innocuously. "I'm going to take a shower before bed. But you go on ahead."

"Okay," I reply.

"Night, Lex," she says.

"Night."

She turns toward the bathroom, but before I can head to the bedroom, I see it out of the corner of my eye. She touches her waist, in the same spot I just touched.

She noticed.

I find my pajamas, still folded in my small oak dresser. Once I've changed, I pull back the sheets and climb into bed. As I settle in, I hear the water run. Only then, when it's safe, do I reach my arm to my right side and run my fingers along the jagged scar forever etched into my body.

That's the thing about scars. You can trick your mind into forgetting, but scars last forever. A visible and permanent reminder of the pain. I've gotten used to the physical scar, but the emotional one is still a gaping wound, sore to even the slightest touch. And seeing Beth today was like taking a cattle prod to it.

I take a deep breath and begin the meditation technique Dr. Greer taught me.

I picture my happy place. It's a meadow in a clearing near our childhood home. Beth is there. Mom and Dad are there. We are only five, or maybe six. We are all happy, lying on a blue-and-red plaid blanket. Mom has set out a massive picnic spread. There are grapes and crackers with cheese, and pink lemonade. Dad is trying to catch a butterfly for us. When he misses, Beth says, "You were just pretending! You weren't really trying," and Mom laughs. I love this memory. I love my happy place. I feel my body begin to relax.

But then, just as I'm on the edge of sleep, I see it. My eyes snap open, but I can't unsee it.

Dad caught the butterfly, but somehow, it's been torn in two and oozes red blood. Mom, Dad, and Beth huddle around it, Beth's long hair like a veil. Their tears fall and dilute the blood. I sit helpless, just as I am now in my bed.

Dr. Greer says it's a metaphor my brain has created to keep a memory I want to get rid of alive. He says I should practice remembering the part of the memory that is *real*, over and over again. I lie back and try a different exercise, knowing full well I'll only dream of murdered butterflies tonight, now that Beth is back.

8

BETH

Warm water rushes over the crown of my head as I stand facing the faucet. My eyes instinctively close, and I let my mind rest. I feel as though I'm watching my brain wander the pathways of my memory. It starts the journey with recent memories, like the feel of the old hardwood floors in Alexa's new apartment under my bare feet, then pings quickly to other, more distant memories. I feel my muscles tense slightly in anticipation as my brain searches itself, and suddenly, I see her. Then my brain pans out like a scene in a movie to reveal the whole picture.

Mom and I are in the kitchen of our old house, although I suppose it's only old to me since I'm the one exiled. Mom is packing a picnic basket with peanut butter and jelly sandwiches for us, tuna salad for her and Dad. I'm at the counter, folding paper towels to use as napkins. I watch as my mom pauses to pull her thick waves of auburn hair into an elastic rubber band.

She looks happy. I miss when we were all happy.

I open my eyes and let the image of our kitchen, lined with

white cabinets, rinse away as I search the shower for shampoo. I know how that memory ends; there's no need to rewatch it. It's like that old movie *Titanic*. Even though I watched it over and over—hoping for the ship to miss the iceberg, for Jack to survive—the ending never changes.

I roll my head around, feeling a pop in my neck before I reach for the Dove body wash tucked in the corner of the tub—it's cucumber-scented. I've never understood the allure of cucumber. I wash my body, taking care when I get to my abdomen. The scar is thirteen years old, but I treat it with the same cautious gentleness as the day my flesh was cut.

As I lather up with body wash, my mind wanders again to that day. To the picnic. It was like any other day, until it wasn't. How can such a happy day turn dark so fast? If only we'd been able to stay in the *before* period, forever.

Annoyed at the emotions bubbling in my brain and body, I crank the faucet to a halt and shove the curtain out of the way—or try to. I have to stop twice to force the rings over the middle part of the curtain rod. As I step out of the tub and reach for the pale gray towel draped over the sink, I look around at the tiny bathroom, and the unavoidable fact flashes in my brain like neon lights on the Vegas Strip. She really did it. She's on her own, just as she always wanted. I try to conjure happiness for my sister, but it doesn't come.

After I finish drying off, I stand in front of the small circular mirror and look at my reflection. People say "I could be looking in a mirror" when they meet someone who shares their features, but as I gaze into the mirror, I think the same concept in reverse. I could be looking at Alexa. It's a bizarre thing for the brain to decode where the line between your own reflection and an entirely different being is blurred. Being a twin is our norm, sure—something we've experienced all our lives—but every once in a while it still comes as a shock when it occurs to me that I am identical to another person. Puts a whole new spin on the old cliché "my other half."

I remind myself why I am here. She needs me—she's always needed me. I try to quiet the second, more truthful part of the sentence away. Or rather, what I like to leave unsaid. I will not admit that I need her too.

9

ALEXA

I'm standing on the subway platform, one dot in a crowd of a dozen or more strangers. Question is, how are there only a dozen people commuting to midtown on this Monday morning? I'm supposed to meet Christine at the office at nine o'clock, so I've built an extra hour into my commute in case I get lost. That way, no matter what, there will still be time to get coffee. A coffee maker is high on the list of things I still need.

Even though I told myself I'd practice the route over the weekend, Beth's surprise arrival ate up most of my spare time. I've obviously ridden the subway many times throughout my life, but never alone, and never to this particular part of midtown. I feel the familiar itch of annoyance toward Beth creep over me.

She's always been particularly adept at ruining any plans I make. In junior high, I wanted to try out for the school's production of *The Grinch*. I practiced religiously, almost 24/7 for three weeks.

On the day of the tryout, I was in the girls' locker room finishing the final touches on my audition piece.

"Be it ever so heinous, there's no place like home," I recited with my best Grinch voice.

Feeling ready, I turned from my locker and ran directly into my sister, who had come to surprise me and wish me luck. The collision knocked me back into the door of an open locker next to mine. I only needed a couple stitches, but I missed the audition and, subsequently, the play.

I check my phone—no signal, but the clock reads 7:49.

I look around the platform again, partly because Dad told me to "keep my head on a swivel for trouble" but also partly out of curiosity.

As if on cue, about a third of my companions inch toward the yellow pebbled line while still looking at their phones. I glance toward the black hole of a tunnel but see nothing. I check the sign above my platform to confirm once more that I'm on the uptown side. When I look back, a faint yellow flame dances in the far depths, and I let out the breath I was holding. A low rumble breaks the stale silence of the platform.

Metal grinds metal as the train slows to a stop. I wait for the doors to open, then step inside the emptiest-looking car. It reeks of urine and some other greasy-food smell.

I take a seat and wait for the doors to close, ignoring the pervasive odor as best I can. I keep my eyes on the subway map, which indicates that our next stop will be Fourteenth Street. The car is cooler than the station, but I'm too on edge to relax.

A few moments later, after the train starts with a jolt, a man walks through a door at the end of the subway car. He saunters the length of this car and through another set of doors, never once acknowledging my sleeping commuter companion sprawled over several seats across from me. I am shocked that the man's so unfazed, passing through as if the sleeper doesn't even exist. I'm equally surprised to discover you can walk between moving cars.

When we stop at the Fourteenth Street station, I decide to follow him into the next car, in pursuit of something less stinky. It's an odd feeling, moving between the cars this way. I don't think I'd like it while the train is moving, and I hurry my steps.

There are no seats here, so I take hold of the vertical pole closest to me and brace myself. New York Subway Lesson Number One: Never Go for the Empty Car.

When we finally arrive at my stop, I release my grip on the pole and exit onto a platform packed with people. I meander through the station, careful to avoid the buzzing masses threatening to knock me over. I follow a herd of people up the concrete steps, through a turnstile, and up another set of steps before the suffocating warmth of the subway gives way to the fresh sunshine and not-so-fresh Manhattan air.

I finally dip my hand into my purse for some sanitizer. Those early days of the pandemic were awful. None of us knew what to think or believe. We couldn't find toilet paper or masks. Liquor companies made hand sanitizer to help with the shortage. But as time in quarantine wore on and we started living in this new normal, we were able to find little silver linings, like all of our favorite restaurants now delivering, new movies straight to our TVs, and morning breath being concealed by masks.

Since the vaccine, we don't have to wear masks anymore, and the restaurants that survived have gone back to their normal business methods—allowing diners to actually dine there—but I still always have hand sanitizer with me. Today, after that trip on the subway, I'm grateful for that pandemic habit.

A loud horn pierces my ears. Several more follow. A wailing

fire engine and the cries of a baby compete for my attention. Doing my best to ignore the jarring noises all around me, I glance at my phone and see that the entire commute took me twenty minutes. I have forty minutes to grab a coffee and get to the office.

"Get the fuck out the way," a fellow New Yorker greets me as he passes. I slip my phone into my bag and begin walking in what I think is a northern direction. I walk half of a block before I see the familiar green mermaid beckoning me to join her for morning coffee. I never have figured out what a mermaid has to do with coffee. Hard to stay awake underwater? Or will drinking coffee make me feel more fresh and alive, like a mermaid?

I duck inside and relish the reprieve from the blaring city soundtrack outside. There are six people ahead of me, so I take out my phone and click the familiar Instagram icon. It's now half past eight, so I have a full thirty minutes to get my coffee and make it upstairs. For the first time today, I take a deep breath, filling my lungs with the aroma of sugar-free syrups and burnt coffee grounds.

After gathering my grande almond-milk latte from the bar, I decide to head up early to meet Christine. The Starbucks opens into a false lobby that's empty except for the eight elevators and some faux plants. I take the escalator to the far left, and it spits me out into the white marble expanse of the real lobby, which has four expertly designed seating areas, a gift shop, a yogurt shop, and a snack bar. A security desk is tucked into the far left corner, guarding the entrance to the next bank of elevators like the guards at Buckingham Palace.

I take a seat on a purple velvet sofa, its color made richer by the sunlight streaming in from the large glass windows. I set my coffee on the Lucite coffee table and am reaching again for my phone when I hear a voice.

"Alexa! You're early! What a great start!" Christine half shouts from the snack shop. She's carrying a short coffee cup in one hand and extending her other, despite the distance still between us.

"Hi! Yes, I didn't want to be late," I say, scrambling for my things so I can stand.

"Oh, girl, the coffee up here is *so* much better. I should have told you," she says, eying my cup with a hint of judgment.

Smiling, I tell her I'm *so* relieved there's something better, but truthfully, I prefer Starbucks to smaller coffee houses. It's my dirty little secret. Well, one of them.

"You ready?" she says, looking me up and down. Immediately, I second-guess the navy knee-length dress and nude heels.

"Yep!"

We make our way toward the guarded turnstiles. She swipes her badge and walks through. "Hey, Steve, this is a new hire—can you swipe her in?"

One of the guards makes his way over and swipes a small iden-tification badge over the reader to unlock the turnstile. His goofy smile indicates that they must have slightly less rigid rules than the Buckingham guards.

Inside an elevator, Christine hits "48" and the doors close.

"We're on forty-nine, but HR is on forty-eight, and we need to stop there first," she explains.

Christine is pretty, not in a Hollywood starlet kind of way but definitely in an East Coast way, with dark, intense features that are softened by the smooth chestnut waves that cascade over her shoul-ders like a cool shawl.

When we reach 48, I follow her through a set of glass doors and notice her heels kick up flashes of red—Christine must be doing well to be wearing Christian Louboutins to commute through New

York City on a random Monday. I've always followed a lot of celeb-rities and influencers on Instagram, but I've upped that since taking the job at FLLW. Most have some version of a photo showing off their red-bottomed shoes. Who knows? Maybe after a few months here, I could get a pair.

We arrive at a corner office with the name "Wendy Bauller" on the placard.

"Knock knock!" Christine sings as she enters.

"Morning, Christine," Wendy replies, looking up from her desk-top screen. She's older, maybe forties, with wild yellow curls that frame her heart-shaped face. Her black frames suggest she lives somewhere cool, like Brooklyn. "You have a nice weekend?" she asks.

"Ugh, I had three dates," Christine laments. "I think I'm going to do a dating cleanse. I just can't with these guys."

Wendy lets out a chuckle laced with sympathy before looking over Christine's shoulder to me. "This must be . . ." She casts a surreptitious glance at a file on her desk. "Alexa?"

"You got it!" Christine steps out of the way and gestures toward me as if offering me up as a bride to a potential suitor in *Game of Thrones*.

"Okay, great." Wendy stands, revealing a slender frame adorned with tight jeans, a white blouse, and a blue blazer. I reach out to take her extended hand before realizing I'm proffering my Starbucks cup.

"No, thanks. I like Ben's in the lobby," she jokes and motions to the same nondescript cup Christine has.

"Oh gosh, sorry," I manage. "I'm a little nervous."

Wendy smiles. "Nothing to be worried about."

"Okay, you two, have fun," Christine says, her nose now buried in her phone. She looks up for long enough to make eye contact with Wendy. "You'll bring her to me when you're all finished, right?"

"You got it. Should be just before lunch."

Once Christine darts out of the door, Wendy passes me a stack of papers she nabs off her desk. "Fill these out, then we'll get you down to security for your badge."

I take the papers in front of me and take a deep breath.

"Don't worry—just the normal HR stuff," she says. "Here, come sit on the couch if you prefer."

She takes the stack from me and carries it, along with my coffee, to the office's sitting area. I sit on the brown leather sofa and place my bag on the floor.

"Ah no!" she shouts, and I jump, wondering how I could possibly have screwed up already. "Never put your purse on the floor, or you'll never be rich!"

I hurriedly move my bag to the sofa. "I didn't know that one."

Wendy laughs and jokingly wipes sweat from her brow, as if to indicate a close call for my finances. "Holler if you have any questions," she says, then retreats to her desk, which is backed by a view of skyscrapers and clouds so perfect it's almost cliché. She sees me looking at her.

"Do you have a pen?" I force out with embarrassment.

"Sure!" she says, reaching into a cup and tossing me one.

I catch the blue ballpoint pen with both hands, then pop the end off and start on the many pages of paperwork.

After what seems like hours, I finish the last signature. As I set the pen down, I open and close my fist to relieve the tension. Wendy has been on some kind of call for the last thirty minutes. I can't gather if it's work related or not, because she only replies with "uh-huh" and "yes" and the occasional "I'm not sure." When she sees me put the pen down, she motions with her index finger and mouths, "One more minute."

Nodding, I sit back and wait. My mind drifts to my sister. What's she going to do all day? She's a big fan of TV, so she'll probably be on the couch watching some reality-show marathon. I know it's possible that she could leave the apartment, but I hope not. Things are always easier when she stays put and out of trouble.

Once Wendy hangs up, she comes over and leafs through the stack of papers. "Okay, looks good. Let's head down to Steve for your badge now."

As we wind through the cubicle maze, passing glass-walled offices and the occasional conference room, Christine comes out of an office with another young blonde woman, curvier than any employee seen here so far, and a young man with green eyes and tan skin who freezes me in my tracks. I feel my heart race.

"We were just on our way to Steve," Wendy says, "but do you need her?"

"Yes! I'd love to have you sit in on this meeting, Alexa," Christine says with a huge smile. "I'll take her down to security right after—promise."

"Okay, sounds good." Wendy starts to head back through the cubicles but then stops. "Welcome to FLLW, Alexa—we're happy to have you on board."

I steady myself and manage to thank her before I turn to follow Christine and my unlikely first client, who are disappearing into a conference room at the end of the hall.

The room is large, way too large for the four of us. He sits at the head of the table. Christine takes the seat to his right, and the curvy blonde, to his left. I'm trying to avoid his eyes by keeping mine locked on Christine. She motions for me to sit next to her. As I take my seat, I'm careful to put my bag on the empty seat next to me rather than the floor.

Christine opens the meeting with some informal introductions, beginning with our new client, Curt Kempton, and then identifying the blonde as Mel, the director of videography, and me as the new marketing assistant on the team. "We love Alexa's perspective on the Gen Z demo because, well, she's Gen Z."

Curt is staring at me, maybe trying to figure out how he knows me. We consume so much media that often we forget who we *know* know and who we just know from TV or the internet. This happened to me with Denzel Washington one time while getting gas in Connecticut. Without thinking, I said hello. He was kind and said hello back, only growing confused when I asked how he'd been. It wasn't until I was pulling out of the station that I realized who he was and that I did not, in fact, know him.

I decide to let Curt lead—don't want to derail my first business meeting with explanations of how I met our client at my therapist's office.

Curt stands and takes my hand in his. "Nice to meet you, Alexa. I'm stoked to see what you have in mind for Phat Food."

He's figured it out. I can see the recognition on his face. But his actions and words direct me to follow.

"I'm stoked to give my ideas," I say, playing along as if we haven't met.

He sits back down and pours himself some water from the pitcher at the center of the table, but he doesn't take a sip.

Christine coughs. "We think the Phat Food channel has so much potential, but we need to get the engagement up. That's why you're here, right?" she asks.

"Yeah." Curt's light green eyes are on me. "I mean, in order to make cash, I need to get *way* more followers."

"But it's really about an active and engaged community," I interject. "And loyalty." The three of them pause and look at me. "Sorry. I just wanted to make sure we highlight how important an authentic following—as opposed to just followers—is for brand longevity."

After I finish, I tell myself this is why they hired me. As someone with a finger on the "pulse of current trends."

"Yes, exactly," Christine says at last.

"Perfect point, Alexa," Mel says. "And a great segue into our overall strategy for you."

What was I thinking, just throwing my ideas out there? The image of my mom flashes in my mind, followed by the memory of the last time I spoke without thinking. One wrong phrase, and Mom died. My heart threatens to jump out of my chest. What just happened cannot happen again, I tell myself. Especially not since Beth is back. I was lucky this time.

Christine has dived right into what I'm guessing is the official pitch they worked up before the meeting. I force myself from my own mind and listen as she outlines the programming for the show, lots of unique recipes, kitchen hacks, and weekly favorite NYC restaurant spotlights. As she drones on and my heart rate recovers, I think about Curt and Phat Foods. When we first met at the Weinstein Center, I thought he was cute. So I went home and looked him up on Instagram and then YouTube. I enjoyed looking through his images and videos, but he didn't have many followers or subscribers. He's handsome and charming, but there are so many food blogs that I can't imagine how we're going to up his engagement enough.

But I'm definitely willing to try if it means spending more time with him.

As the meeting comes to a close, I file out behind the rest of the group. Nerves have my skin prickling like lightning. I decided to let Curt lead, but am I really supposed to pretend that him being here isn't an amazing coincidence? Or maybe it's fate, even. Do I really want to ignore fate?

Much to my excitement, as we're finishing up the goodbyes, Christine says, "Alexa, will you please walk Curt to the elevators?"

"Sure," I say calmly, fully in control. "Follow me."

We wind around the corner toward the set of glass doors. I can feel his eyes on me the whole way.

"Well, I think that went well," he says.

"Yes. I think there's a lot we can do to help," I reply, knowing I'm lying, waiting for him to acknowledge the mounting elephant in the room. He reaches for the glass door and motions for me to go first. I counter by pressing the down arrow. It's possible we'll both play chicken forever and never acknowledge our past moments.

"Alexa, I think it's best we don't let them know how we know each other," he says finally.

Even though I came to this conclusion on my own, this rankles. "Of course. This is my first job, and I really want to do well."

"Would you be comfortable keeping one more secret then?" he asks, swiveling his head around to make sure we're still alone.

"It depends," I say honestly. I *really* don't like secrets.

"Well, I've wanted to ask you to dinner for a while now, but you seemed spooked last time I saw you. But it seems destiny keeps trying to bring us together. So what do you say?"

Wow. I can't believe he finally asked me. I've been lingering and even showing up early sometimes to my appointments with Dr. Greer, just hoping to run into him more.

"I'd like that," I manage coolly.

"Great. We can keep that as our little secret."

The ding of the elevator grabs both of our attention. All I see is Curt's smile as the doors close, but my brain is screaming. Why did he say I seemed spooked? Did I act weird when we saw each other last? I rack my brain for the details of our last run-in and come up empty.

A massive smile sweeps across my face as I head back into the office. Curt asked me out.

This, for once, is a secret I'm happy to keep.

10

BETH

The buzzer wakes me from the coma of boredom I've been in while Alexa has been at work. I don't know how the housewives on TV do it. All day, hour after hour, with no purpose. No adventure. I may not be the epitome of a career-obsessed *Boss Babe*, but at least I know how to have fun. And my existence on this planet is certainly an adventure.

You're here for Alexa, I remind myself as I make my way toward the intercom. I don't even bother to ask who's there; I simply hit the four buttons, since I've yet to decipher which one actually opens the door. I release them after a few seconds, and the buzzer sounds again. Idiot. I press all the buttons once more and hold them this time.

I release them and listen for another buzz, but it's silent. I make my way to the door.

The delivery man's almost a foot shorter than me, dressed in a full yellow rain outfit that hides everything except his gloved hands. I take the wet bag—I hadn't even realized it was raining.

That's the thing about the city; it's so loud you can't even hear the rain. I miss the sound of late afternoon summer storms and raindrops pitter-pattering on our suburban roof. *Their* suburban roof, I correct myself. I wonder if the residents on the top floor of these skyscrapers can hear the rain, while the rest of the occupants are only played the drumming and tapping of their upstairs neighbors' feet.

Our house was modest, but its location afforded it prestige. Alexa and I always shared a room, leaving the one guest room mostly vacant. Mom's parents died when we were in middle school. They had Mom when they were older, so we were the first of all our friends to lose grandparents. And Dad's parents died when a drunk semi-truck driver hit them head-on. Mom was the youngest of her five siblings, and we hardly ever saw our uncles and aunt—but it wasn't anything traumatic that we weren't the family with a dozen or so members at a Sunday meal. Our family was small, and we liked it that way.

I open the plastic bag first, then carefully lift the contents of the brown paper bag onto the coffee table. Alexa and I rarely ordered takeout growing up, but from what I can tell, the city has more options than the local pizza joint and one Chinese restaurant in our sleepy town. As I take the containers out of the wet bag, I see there are five fortune cookies at the bottom. I reach in and lift them out, feeling the shame of the restaurant's judgment. Or obliviousness. Two entrees, and they think there are five of us dining? There are so many different flavors on their menu it's nearly impossible to select one. Thankfully, the shame passes quickly when I find the fried rice.

After several moments spent contemplating the great fork-or-chopsticks debate, I settle on the fork and make my way to the lonely kitchen drawer where it lives. It's not like the utensil drawer at home, with dividers and a proper matching set. There's plenty here for Lex to be comfortable enough, but it definitely screams "this is my first apartment." I force myself to squash the judgment. It's not as though I'm a winning homemaker. I close the drawer and turn back through the small doorless doorframe. To my surprise, Alexa is already sitting on the couch, shoes kicked off at her feet. Her bag is on the other cushion of the loveseat. Her hair is not as wet as I expected—it must have stopped raining.

"Hey, big boss lady, how was the first day?" I say with a carefully modulated amount of sisterly pride and animation.

"Great!" she replies. "Long day, though. I am going to have to get used to that."

"I bet!" I exclaim. "I ordered Chinese again."

She opens the bag and selects a carton and set of chopsticks. I love the way my sister's brain works—she's always been better at making decisions than me, even when it comes to the small stuff.

"What did you get?" she asks with a mouthful of broccoli beef.

"Fried rice. I was thinking we could split, so go easy over there. Looks like someone worked up an appetite."

"Yeah, I missed lunch because I got pulled into my first client meeting," she says without lifting her gaze from the food.

"Oh, wow," I reply.

"Yeah, it's this badass YouTuber who's looking to increase engagement," she says.

"Is he cute?" I ask, hoping for the story to get interesting.

"Yeah, I guess. He's a YouTuber, so he's obviously going to be attractive. But better yet, he liked my ideas." She shares with the same smile she had when she told me Tommy Restik was going to ask her to prom. My brain pings. *She's not telling me something.*

"Look at you. So, what's his name? Let's look him up."

Without waiting for an answer, I head for the bedroom, where she keeps her laptop on the purple nightstand. There are still boxes in the corner.

"K, name, please?" I ask as I open her computer.

She's staring at me, and I realize that she's seen me put in her password. Oops. Surprisingly, she doesn't say anything. But I can tell she's annoyed.

"Name?" I demand.

"No," she replies with a sigh. "He's a client, and I can't share client info."

"I'm sorry, did you become a doctor? Or a lawyer? Or a shrink?" I pester. "Because last time I checked, client confidentiality doesn't apply to people who literally put their lives on the internet."

"I'm new—I don't know how it works, but my boss told me not to gossip about clients outside of the office."

She's lying. But why?

"Alexa. It's me. Who am I going to tell?"

"I don't know . . . Can't I just keep work stuff at work?"

"No. You're being so annoying. Just tell me his freaking blog or whatever."

"Fine. You're relentless. Just go to YouTube and type 'Phat Food,'" she directs, with visible unease.

As I begin to type what she's told me, the lame pun registers. "Phat Food? Really?"

"Yeah, it's pretty popular," she counters. "He just needs to grow his social following to get better partnership deals, and maybe even his own TV show or cookbook."

I roll my eyes and laugh.

"Just do it," she directs, gesturing at the laptop.

I type the most idiotic brand name ever known to man into the search bar of the YouTube home page and watch as far too many videos featuring a mediocre-looking blond man in a T-shirt fill the page. I click one titled "Phat Food: Pho Real."

My sister was always a sucker for a blond guy.

The video starts with a black page listing only the author's full name: Curt Kempton. Next, we see the man I assume is Curt in some kitchen not much larger than Alexa's, although his does have a microwave. He's wearing what I think is a vintage shirt from Coachella. There are at least a dozen bowls on the counter, each in a different color.

"Who's ready to make some Phat Pho?" he says, and I snicker under my breath. But Alexa is transfixed, watching Mr. Phat Food with the admiration she shows as a Belieber.

I'm about to make a sarcastic comment about the low production value and overall stench of this cheeseball when she speaks.

"That looks bomb," she says sincerely. "We need to up his production value, but honestly, Beth, that's what people are into right now. Authenticity."

Clearly, Alexa has a crush. I hesitate, remembering all the crushes Alexa's been crushed by—after all, that's what always happens—and I realize there's no need for me to crush her when this douchebag YouTuber certainly will. What was that kid's name in junior year? Mark something, I think. Only one week into "going out," he dumped her on an Instagram Live. She was so mortified that she faked being sick for almost a week, to avoid showing her face at school. And they didn't even share any classes. I wonder if she ever found out what I said to him.

I click another video.

We watch only two more—it's all I can bear. But then something hits me—he looks familiar. I stare at him while he talks into the camera, but I can't figure it out.

"Does he look familiar to you?" I ask.

"What do you mean?" she counters.

"I mean, does he look familiar to you? As in, have we met him before?"

"No. I don't think so," she says before adding, "I just met him today."

Maybe he has one of those familiar faces, I reason with myself as Lex drones on and on about Phat Food and its captain, Curt. But it's not just his face. It's his voice and mannerisms. I can't place it, and it's making me feel oddly uncomfortable, so I coax my sister into letting me put down the laptop and watch an old episode of *The Kardashians* instead.

But as Khloé and Kourtney work out at one of their home tennis courts, my attention drifts to the only window in the apartment. The rain has definitely subsided, but the pattern it's left on the window transfixes me.

And it hits me—in my trancelike state—the memory of another male voice ordering someone back to the kitchen.

"Curt, drop those and help get these onions chopped for lunch."

Alexa's new boyfriend works at the Weinstein Center. She lied to me.

11

ALEXA

The sun shines brightly through the window, urging me out of bed before my alarm has the chance to do its job. I used to dread the morning sun, but something's shifted since I started at FLLW. I shove the obvious thought to the back of my mind.

It's not because of Curt. It's because I'm finally living my life.

In the living room, I tiptoe past the lump of blankets that is Beth on the sofa and into the bathroom. I start the shower and look in the mirror, and I'm startled at the smile and lightness that beams back at me. As I step into the tub and under the warm water, I picture the way Curt's hair curls, the lines that frame his wide smile. And then there's the broadness of his shoulders.

I'm interrupted from my daydreaming by the feeling of water starting to fill the tub around my ankles. Hurriedly rinsing the soap from my hair and body, I twist the rusted chrome knob all the way to the right. Once I've wrapped the white cotton towel around me, I dip my hand into the tub and search for the drain, only to find that it's already open.

Using one hand to brace myself on the side of the tub, I dig inside. I have the majority of my fingers in the drain when I feel something small but hard, wrapped in what I presume is hair. I shimmy the clog up the drain and finally pull the object out of the water, which quickly disappears down the now-clear pathway.

Carefully, I start to pick away the strands of hair, and as I do, an object emerges. Shocked, I sit down on the toilet seat. The sapphire ring belonged to Mom. After she passed away, Beth and I sorted through her items, and I kept this—our mother's engagement ring. Mom never wore it, but I loved the uniqueness of the deep blue stone ringed by tiny diamonds. I slip the ring onto my finger and force a deep breath, despite the mounting tension in my body.

There's only one way this ring ended up here. If she's already rifling through my things, she must suspect that I still have the journal.

Dr. Greer has explained, ad nauseum, how traumatic experiences or accidents often leave the victims feeling decidedly different, or *changed*, but Beth's taken it to an extreme ever since the incident. Mom certainly thought so. Sometimes she'd watch Beth with a frown, as if trying to puzzle out exactly what move she'd make next.

She needed to, given the last one put me in the hospital.

That year, when we were nine, I spent two weeks in a sterile white bed, in and out of consciousness after numerous surgeries. Mom cried while Dad clung to the walls as if scared to be without them propping him up, only moving to go and fetch nurses. When I'd healed enough to stay awake for hours at a time, I spent days asking to see Beth, only to finally be told that I wouldn't be seeing her for a while. "One day, baby girl," Mom told me. "One day."

I drift back to my bathroom, feeling the light weight of the ring on my finger.

When I did finally see Beth again, she was different.

The thing is, I don't think I am different. If it weren't for everyone else telling me how *different* I am, I'd be none the wiser. Since that moment, I've been trying to make sense of what they see.

12

BETH

When I wake up, Alexa is gone. I'm not sure why she insists on leaving hours before work, but if I had to guess, it's likely her need to control. That's the thing about this city: You can't control anything. Not the subways, not the people, not the traffic, weather, nothing. So my sister leaves three hours before work to ensure that she won't fall prey to the city's game.

Control.

Truthfully, I love mornings. Alexa's never been a fan, but there's something about their stillness that I enjoy, the peace that one finds before the day inevitably ruins itself. Sunrises are my favorite.

Not that I can really see one out the window of this sardine can. Right now, at six o'clock, there are only a few people out and about. I watch them and wonder, *What's your secret?* In the city that never sleeps, it seems that many do, in fact, sleep until about nine. But these rare few, what brings them out so early? I want to know. Are they just coming home? Are they leaving early? Where are they going, and what have they done?

We have always been curious, Alexa and I. I think it's because of all the doctor's visits and our *unique* situation. When you're not "normal," it makes you extra curious.

I retreat to the sofa as the morning sun coaxes the rest of the city's *normal* people out onto its streets. I open Alexa's laptop and immediately search for more of Curt's videos. I don't like him. But I'm not sure why yet. I don't like that he works at Weinstein, and I really don't like that Alexa is pretending she's just met him at work—from the way he acted that day at the center, it's clear that they met before he became a FLLW client.

I click on a video titled "A Night in Tuscany." A pre-roll ad for a new Lexus plays for fifteen seconds before I'm allowed to skip it. After the boring black screen, Curt's banal voice drones on and on about the flavors of Italy and the health benefits of tomatoes. I take a break to make a cup of coffee, then almost choke on my fresh brew as I hear him pronounce bruschetta as *brew-sket-ah*, complete with phony Italian accent. It even drives me nuts when Giada De Laurentiis pronounces dishes in Italian, and she is Italian, allegedly. And Guy Fieri (Fee-air-e, as he says) was born Guy Ferry. Like the ferry to Staten Island. Why can't these people just be who they really are? Curt *looks* Scandinavian but talks like he's from Staten Island. And he has the same fake-for-TV persona they all do.

I close the laptop and turn on the TV to look for anyone besides Giada and Guy.

My days haven't been particularly full recently. I'm not working, dating has never been a priority, and Dad won't acknowledge me. Alexa's always been my best friend, but now she's busy. This "waiting around for your sister to come home" thing gets boring. If I ever do date and marry, I don't think I'll be able to be a housewife. At least not in the traditional sense—the Bravo sense still seems doable.

I think about making a trip to her office to check in, but decide against it. A *Real Housewives of Atlanta* marathon lures me in for far too long. A woman named Nene is yanking the shirt of a cameraman when I hear the door again. I check the clock and realize I've consumed seven hour-long episodes. I sit up and try to act as though I haven't been in the same place since she left this morning.

"Hello?" she says as she closes the door and hangs her keys.

"Hey, working girl. How was it today?"

"Good! Busy. The day flew by."

"I know! Me too," I tell her, and it's true, thanks to Nene and her friends. "So, any interaction with Mr. Phat?"

"Yeah!" She smiles wistfully, tucking her hair behind her ears and out of her face. I'm completely unfamiliar with her growing confidence.

"Actually, he came into the office again today for a strategy meeting."

"Cool. Any hope for him?" I say with fake interest.

"I know you think he's lame, but he's got a growing audience in the micro food vlogging community," she counters. "*And* we're going out tonight."

A part of me sinks at that. I'm too late. He's got his hooks in her already.

I struggle with what to say next. "Oh. Isn't that, uh . . ."

"Unprofessional? It's 2021, Beth."

"What about the #MeToo movement?"

She's getting angry. I can feel it in my gut.

"Stop," she says. "It's fine." After a moment, her tone softens. "Will you be okay on your own?"

"I'm fine on my own, thank you," I say, gesturing to my current existence with a Vanna White wave of my arm. "But I will absolutely not lie if you do any kind of misconduct of the type that gets men in trouble. Women can be the offenders too. Look at those teachers in Texas who keep sleeping with their students."

I've made her laugh despite herself.

"You're insane," she says indulgently.

"No, you are."

As soon as the words are out of my mouth, I realize what I've said. I quickly debate acknowledging my reflexive response, but before I can come to a decision, it seems she's chosen to ignore it. The whole Dr. Greer psych ward thing makes her very sensitive to any words in the "insane" family. I feel a little remorse. I've had to endure these too, obviously, but it never bothered me like it did her.

"I'm going to freshen up because he should be here soon," she says as she heads toward her room.

"He's coming here?" I say, sitting taller than I have all day.

She stops at the door and turns to face me. She gives me a look as if I've said something ridiculous. "Well, not up. Just to pick me up. Like outside."

I'm relieved. I'm not ready to deal with him yet.

"Look, Lex . . . can I talk to you super fast?" I ask.

"Beth, I am going out with him. Can you please drop the over-protective sister thing and let me just have this? Please?" she begs.

"I just don't know about him," I begin.

"Beth. Please? Just this once, can you trust me?" she says.

And there it is. She and I both know why I can't and don't trust her. And why she doesn't trust me either.

"Lex. I saw him at Weinstein," I blurt.

That makes her go still.

"When?" she asks.

"I saw him in the dining room when I was grabbing a snack

trying to find my way through that checkerboard hell to Dr. G," I tell her. "I think he works there, in the kitchen or something." I wait for her to react.

"Yeah, he does," she says, all nonchalant, as she struggles to get her foot into a leather boot.

"What? You knew him before?"

My sister's been hiding things from me.

"I didn't know him that well. We just talked a few times. But I was genuinely surprised when he came in as our client."

"That's so weird," I say. "I mean, that he works at our therapist's office."

"No, it's not. Do you know how hard it is to be profitable as a vlogger?" she retorts. "Literally every influencer has to have, like, five side hustles to pursue their craft."

"Their *craft*?"

She prickles. "You don't have to like him or his vlog, but you do have to back off," she snaps. "He's a good guy and he likes me."

"Right. Because he doesn't know you."

That hurts her, I can tell. But that's the thing about Alexa—she doesn't let people know her, then acts as though it's your fault when you do.

"He knows more than you think," she threatens.

My body goes cold at that. No. Fucking. Way.

"How much, Alexa?" I ask sternly.

She doesn't respond.

"What does he fucking know, Alexa? What have you told him?" I say with even more firmness.

"Not that. Relax," she says. "He just knows that I'm in therapy, and he doesn't judge me for it. He's a patient there too."

With that, she disappears into the other room.

I sit on the sofa and feel rage build inside of me. This guy cannot know her secrets. Alexa's been so great at keeping things quiet, but letting this Curt get close will threaten everything we've worked to keep safe. If she believes this Curt character loves the *real* her, she's delusional. Once he knows what she did, he'll be gone.

Or, worse, he'll expose us both. To the whole world, on one of his vlogs.

I walk toward her room and make my way across the small space to stand behind my sister, who is seated on a tiny stool at her vanity. She's pinning her hair back into a low messy bun, and I look at her through the mirror. She looks pretty.

"Alexa, he cannot ever know. You know that, right?" I say, this time with more kindness.

"I know. Jesus, how dumb do you think I am?" she snaps back.

"I don't think you're dumb, but you have to be careful."

"I know. Please just leave me alone."

"I know that's what you've always wanted, but sorry, sis, that's not the cards you were dealt," I snap back. "And let me remind you, Alexa, you *owe* me."

Her eyes drop to her hands. "I know," she says softly, twisting something around her finger. I realize it's Mom's ring.

"So, you found it?" I say.

She stops but doesn't look up at me. I keep my eyes fixed on our mom's ring. I took it after she died, even though Lex went batshit saying she'd claimed it first. No matter—I gave it to Lex when I left for treatment. A reminder of all we have survived. All of the pain. All of the secrets. Maybe that was what compelled me to stick it down the drain.

"Why did you come here?" she finally asks.

I don't respond. Instead, I pick up a bobby pin from the vanity and secure the last loose end of her bun.

"We had a deal. I held up my end. I just need to make sure you hold up yours," I tell her.

"You still don't trust me after all these years. I've literally done everything you've wanted. What else do I have to do?"

"Don't go out with him," I say.

"No. I'm not going to stop living because you're afraid. I won't do it," she argues back, right before she realizes what she's said.

"I'd never want you to stop living your life, Lex," I say. "I've given so much up so you could."

I leave before she can respond. She follows me out to the living room but says nothing. We both know the weight of her words.

I pick up the remote and confirm that there are five more episodes of *Real Housewives* coming up. I know it's supposed to rot your brain to watch this much TV, but I've done worse things. I turn the volume up and force myself to transport back to Atlanta.

She grabs her purse from the sofa and looks at me, but I don't look back at her.

"I'll be back soon," she says.

"I thought he was coming to get you. I didn't hear the buzzer."

"He just texted to meet him instead. He's already there waiting for a table to open up." She tries again: "Please don't worry."

I stay silent, eyes fixed on Nene, resisting the urge to jab at his lack of manners.

The door opens and shuts, and I hear the loud click of the deadbolt. I cannot believe she went. She never goes against my wishes. Well, not since the incident at least. I know I have to figure out a way to get rid of Curt, but for now, I sit back and hope his boring and surely self-indulgent conversation will be enough to do the trick.

"Wrong road. Wrong road," sings from a character on the TV, and I temporarily vacate my present reality.

~

Hours pass and she's still not back. I've been on the internet for a while now, and I can't find anything damning on Curt. Apparently, he went to rehab, but who hasn't? He had some minor brushes with the law for shoplifting and trespassing, but those pale in comparison to my own rap sheet. None of this will faze Alexa.

As I'm setting the laptop on the coffee table, I catch sight of my chipped black nail polish. It looks terrible. I decide that a brief break from this project won't hurt. I head to the bathroom and search the tiny medicine cabinet for nail polish and remover, but I don't find anything. I move my search to the kitchen cabinets, but they're bare.

In Alexa's room, I start with her dresser, then the closet. I push past some newer items that I'm guessing are a recent office-attire splurge. Alexa has always had a more vanilla sense of style than me. Then I see it. The black cotton dress. It was the last thing Mom wore before she died—we couldn't keep the shirt and pants she wore *when* she died since they were stained. I push the memory of Mom out of my mind and keep searching. I come up empty. Where is it?

I finally tear into the boxes in the corner she still hasn't unpacked. I dig through our old toys, clothes, and some other trinkets, but nothing groundbreaking. I move to the second box and find books, a couple of old board games, and the hideous Raggedy Ann doll from Grandma. I can't believe she's kept this crap.

I'm about to give up when I see it. I reach into the box and pull it out. My stomach turns. Why hasn't she destroyed this yet? This small, unassuming little book ties all of our secrets together.

I hate this diary. And I hate that I've caught her in another lie. This is not one that I can just let go.

13

ALEXA

With each clack of my heel on the stone steps down to the lobby, I try to force thoughts of Beth away. She's always been protective of me, despite my being perfectly capable of taking care of myself. Neither of us has ever really dated, so I wasn't sure how she'd act, but I should have expected this. Still, no matter how angry and annoyed I am right now, I won't let her ruin this date.

I'm on the second-floor landing when a voice startles me.

"Hi," says a woman standing in front of her doorway with a bag of groceries. She's older, but not grandma-old. Maybe my dad's age. Slight wrinkles curl around her eyes and mouth. She's pretty.

"Oh. Hi," I respond, searching for a name that's clearly not in my brain. "How are you?"

"Oh, good. Headed out?"

"Yes. A date, actually." I can't hide my wide grin.

"A date?" she says with a look of deep concern that I was not expecting. Beth must have spoken with her at some point but not explained that we're twins. It feels odd to go into that now, and in any case, I don't have the time.

"Yes, actually," I say, and I feel the smile take a more normal shape.

"Ah! Really? Well, good for you, anyhow. I'm glad you've had a change of heart." She lets out a little nervous laugh. "I guess this means I can worry a little less about our male tenants getting picked on!"

"Oh, well . . . I was having one of those days. You know— where you just don't like men very much."

"I certainly do. You have fun now, dear."

A change of heart? Male tenants getting picked on? I can only imagine what it was that Beth said to her.

She disappears into her apartment before I can try to prod for more clarity. I decide to shrug it off and continue down the stairs to the lobby.

Outside, the darkness of night paints the sky. The buildings in the West Village are smaller than those of midtown or even uptown, where skyscrapers block out the sky. I can't see any stars or the moon, but no one can see stars in New York City—or in a lot of cities, I imagine. The city lights outshine the stars. It's actually a little sad.

The restaurant Curt chose is only three blocks from my apartment, but I need all three to fully evict Beth's judgy voice. I almost miss the entrance because it's unassuming, or it would be were it not for the flow of people entering and exiting through the navy-blue door. I've seen savvy New Yorkers post about L'Artusi on Instagram, but I've never been. When Curt proposed the hip Italian eatery for our date, I was elated. I didn't tell Beth this detail—she would have been jealous. Or worse, she would have come to "check in" on me and the restaurant. It was easier to say he was picking me up, so that she would be focused on that rather than where I was going.

There is a literal wall of people blocking the door. I am too timid to make my way to the hostess stand, so instead, I tuck myself into the corner by the bar and wait for him. As I stand against the wall, someone presses up against my side, and the weight of a human body there once again makes me suddenly dizzy.

It's a few moments before I realize that the new presence is Curt.

"Hi! You look great," Curt says, leaning in more. When I make no move to respond, he hugs me.

I force myself to recover with a nod and smile. The sensation in my side dulls, and my heart slows to a normal speed. I feel the softness of his black-and-red flannel against my bare arms.

"Grab my hand," he directs when he pulls away, so I do. We walk to the hostess stand, Curt like a human shield paving the way.

"Curt!" the hostess exclaims. Her thick brown curls bounce as she makes her way around the stand. "Right this way."

She leads us through the small restaurant with ease, taking us to a staircase. As we climb the steps, I get a proper look at Curt. He's wearing dark, fitted jeans and white sneakers that look as if they're glowing against the black staircase. He turns to smile at me, and his smile is so wide I feel as if it's at least fifty percent responsible for his popularity in the influencer space. It's warm and framed by strong, defining angles.

The staircase brings us to a small loft-type space with only five tables. They're all full except one in the corner that overlooks the restaurant.

"Your usual table," the hostess says, and even though she's pulling the chair out for me, she's smiling at Curt. He thanks her, and she tells us to "Enjoy."

"Wow. You must be pretty special to get this kind of treatment," I say.

"I washed dishes here for two years in high school."

"Ah, well . . . still. It's impressive." I've heard stories of restaurants in NYC and the difficulty of getting a table.

"You get what you give," he says with another smile before opening the wine list. "Do you prefer red or white?"

If I'm honest, I never drink much. With all the different medications, Dr. Greer's always advised against it. Plus, I've only been of legal drinking age for a little over a year, and Dad was never the kind of parent to let us drink wine with dinner.

"I'm fine with anything, really," I say.

"They have this incredible Lambrusco. You have to try it. It's perfect for the summer."

I have no idea what Lambrusco is, but I tell him I would love to try it. A waitress in a white button-down shirt and apron appears. Curt orders the wine and a bottle of still water. I'm more of a tap water person, but I'm assuming he'll be paying. When she disappears with our drink order, I turn my attention from the menu to Curt.

"What do you recommend, Chef?" I ask.

"Chef?" he exclaims with laughter.

"Yes! What does the professional recommend here?"

"Well, I'm certainly trying, but I'm not at professional status yet. Once I hit one million followers, then it will be official."

"We'll get you there," I say. I'm still unsure about the right balance of professionalism and flirting to bring to this date.

"I hope so," he says. "But as far as recommendations go, I love the burrata as a starter, and the bucatini is out of this world."

"Sounds good to me," I say, even though I'm not sure what either are. My Italian cuisine experience stops at pizza and spaghetti.

When the waitress returns, Curt places our order. Afterward, we continue our conversation, mostly about Curt and his travels. I had no idea he'd been to so many places—no wonder he loves food from so many cultures! I assumed it was a New York thing, but it's becoming apparent that it's a Curt thing.

I'm envisioning Croatia, with its quaint stone streets and grand castles perched high atop cliffs overlooking the Adriatic Sea, when he dramatically shifts subjects.

"So, enough about me—tell me about your family."

I freeze. I hate this topic. What can I tell him that won't sound horrific? His face tells me I'm taking too long to respond, so I scramble for an answer.

"Well, it's just me and Dad now. So there's not much to share."

"No siblings? Has your mom passed away?" he prods.

"It's a long story. Why don't you tell me about your family?" I redirect, and he takes the bait.

I learn that Curt has three brothers, two who live on the West Coast and one who lives in London. His parents are still happily married and live on Staten Island. He tells me about how close they are, and I feel a familiar sting at my side. Moving slowly beneath the table, I feel the raised jagged edges of my scar beneath my silky tank. Scars are pain's way of demanding to be remembered. Pain is fleeting, but a scar is forever.

It's a welcome distraction when the server drops the burrata on the table. We devour it, then the bucatini and even a little slice of flourless chocolate cake for dessert. The bill comes, and Curt grabs it before I can react. Once he signs, we stand and make our way for the door. It's less crowded now, revealing the quaint restaurant's full charm. Curt thanks the hostess, and I thank her too as we step outside.

I've been debating how to say goodbye since dessert. Truthfully, I wish it didn't have to be over.

"Can I walk you home?" he says, and it surprises me.

"Yes!" I say a little too quickly. He must not want this date to end yet either.

We walk the few blocks back to my building. Unfortunately, I can't invite him in because Beth is upstairs.

"Thank you for coming out with me tonight. I had a good time," he says, grabbing my hand. "I'd like to see you again."

"Well, we have that meeting tomorrow," I remind him with a wink.

He smiles. "I mean outside of FLLW."

I smile back. "Me too."

He leans in to hug me, and I feel his lips on my cheek. Slowly, his lips graze a path to mine. When they touch, butterflies erupt. I have only kissed a handful of people and only *kiss* kissed two. Following his lead, I only step back when he pulls away. He smiles and leans in once more to kiss my forehead.

"See you tomorrow," he says.

"Yes. Goodnight," I manage.

He turns and walks away, and I open the front door to my building. As I ascend the stairs, I steel myself for another fight with my sister.

14

BETH

I stand with my face pressed against the only window in the bedroom, watching for Alexa. The street is relatively quiet despite the sounds that call from other parts of the city. A man turns the corner, talking on his cell phone loud enough for me to catch a few words. I wait and watch others pass, but none are Alexa.

Finally, I see her. No, *them*. When they stop outside our front door, I will them to say their quick goodbyes. But they linger. I watch as he leans in and then kisses my sister. I hit the glass with an open palm and quickly regret the reflex. But they didn't hear. They're too wrapped up in each other.

Yuck.

What feels like five entire minutes passes before my sister detaches herself from his grip. I watch her walk to the door before I reclaim my seat on the sofa. I want to warn her, but instead I hear strange words leave my mouth: "Hey, Lex! How was it?"

"It was actually really nice."

She keeps walking toward her room. I wait a moment, then

decide to follow her. She's already stripped off her date-night outfit and replaced it with the old torn gray sweatshirt and sweatpants.

"Well, tell me about it," I say, slipping under the covers next to her.

"He's really cool and interesting—and kind of a celebrity around town." She smiles, her mind very obviously drifting back to a happy memory from the evening.

"A celebrity, huh? Well, that must be fun."

"Yeah, the restaurant was packed, but they seated us right away. I guess he used to work there or something." She rolls to face me. "Don't you think that says something about a person? The way people from their past treat them?"

I'm not completely sure where she's going with this.

She continues. "Like, he must be a good guy if his old colleagues still treat him well. He can't have burned too many bridges, you know?"

Colleagues? You've got to be kidding me. "Oh, yeah. Probably not," I manage, but my mind is already on the diary. Or rather, *still* on the diary. "Why'd you keep it, Lex?"

"Keep what?"

"The diary. I found it earlier when I was looking for nail polish."

She looks down to my nails, and I watch the chain of thoughts connect. Clearly, I never found any nail polish.

"I keep it because if I throw it away, someone could find it," she says.

"I just think we need to get rid of it. Burn it. Destroy it."

"Why? It's safe with me, Beth. I promise."

"You said that last time, and look what trouble it caused."

She stares at me, her face like a stone sculpture, unmoving but alive. I know she's there too, in that horrible moment when we first were caught.

That day, I heard her crying before I even entered our room.

When I did, she sat up from where she'd been lying facedown, fresh tears still making their way down her cheeks.

"She knows," she said.

"You told her?"

"No! She found the diary."

"How?"

"I don't know. I just found her in here reading it."

"She read it? All of it?"

"Yes. I think all of it. And she just kept asking about you. But I didn't tell her anything."

I felt the panic rise as I searched my brain for a plan. But then I heard her say the worst part: "Beth, she took it."

"Jesus, Alexa. Why do you have to write everything down?"

"You have no idea what this is like. I feel insane."

"Well, now I'll have to deal with this."

We sat in silence for a couple of minutes before we heard Mom calling us for dinner.

At the table, both of our parents were quiet. Mom kept her head down, clearly trying to fight back tears. Finally, Dad asked us how our days were. I could tell his casualness was genuine. She hadn't shown him the diary yet.

Suddenly, Mom looked at Alexa.

"Tell me what is happening with you and Beth," she demanded with an eerie calm. I froze, willing Alexa to keep her mouth shut. Or at least to come up with a good lie.

When we said nothing, Mom started to cry. Dad got up to hug her, his face painted with confusion.

"What is going on?" he demanded.

"She needs to go back to the hospital," my mom howled. "The meds aren't working. She needs more help . . . something different maybe."

I feel the anger boil, now, as it did then. I refuse to go back to that place. I will not.

"Can I please be excused?" Alexa finally said, then we left the table before anyone could grant permission. It was a little win for me—I had long been working on Alexa to assert herself, to not cave to their every demand.

Back in our room, she started crying again, so I sat on the bed and held her. She was finally starting to stop when Dad opened the door. He sat next to Alexa and placed his hand on her shoulder.

"You can talk to me," he told us. "You can always talk to me."

But when we said nothing, Dad rubbed his head and then retreated. Shortly after, I heard the sound of the garage door open and close. Starting after the accident, Dad would often go to the local sports bar, where he'd stick to three beers and a round of pool before coming home. Mom was always in bed before he got back, but I don't think she slept.

I turned to Alexa and told her to stay put.

"Where are you going?" she said, panicked.

"Just stay put—I'll be back in a couple minutes."

I made my way to the kitchen, where Mom was still sitting at the table, although she'd traded the dirty dishes for a pile of bills. Her back was toward me. As I raised the handgun, a stillness took over me, and I only took one quiet breath before I fired the bullet into her temple.

There wasn't as much blood as I'd imagined. She'd dropped forward over her bills, and that was where she was when I placed the gun in my mother's hand.

"I'm sorry," I whispered.

"What did you *do*?"

Alexa's voice sounded as though it was coming from miles away. I turned to find her watching me.

"Call the police!" I told her.

But she didn't move.

"Call the police," I told her again. When she still didn't move, I grabbed the phone myself and dialed 9-1-1 before shoving it in her hand and telling her exactly what to do.

Our mother killed herself—at least that was the official story—and everyone believed it. "Poor Carrie. The accident was just too much for her to deal with anymore," I heard one of Mom's book club ladies say at the funeral, and another in the group sympathized with her. "I cannot imagine living through something like that."

I don't think our father wanted to think of any other possibilities. I had long found and hidden the diary just in case, but he still ended up exiling me to the center anyway. Alexa had to go too, but she was able to leave after only a few weeks.

I never thought that Alexa would figure out where to find the diary, but clearly she dug it up in our room when she was released. Why did she keep it?

Now, I watch as Alexa's face grows panicked. She gets up and starts to pace.

"I'll get rid of it, okay? I promise."

"I don't understand why you kept it."

"It's not all bad in there. I want to remember some things exactly how they happened, and reading them is the best way," she explains. "Even Dr. Greer says so."

"Okay, but you know, he's not the authority on—"

"Plus, I miss her," she adds.

My stomach flips. I miss her too sometimes. But I've been without any of them far longer than Alexa. I stay quiet as she lies back down and turns her back toward me. I rub it until her heartrate settles and her fear gives way to sleep.

Quietly, I slip out from under the covers and go to the living room, where I pull out Alexa's laptop and get back to work on my plan. I need to keep Curt away from Alexa. If she trusts him, if she thinks they're similar, she may slip and tell him the secret. Or, worse, *he* could find the diary. I make a note to destroy it in the morning when Alexa is at work. I may not be able to stop my sister from telling our secrets, but I can at least destroy the evidence.

I close the laptop after an hour of internet sleuthing. I consider myself to be a pretty decent amateur investigator, so I'm disappointed that I can't find anything damning on Curt. I was, however, served several ads for Ann Taylor LOFT, so at least I've identified where some of Alexa's new looks came from. As I set the laptop on the coffee table, I see my nails once again. I make another mental note to get them done tomorrow, and then I lie back on the sofa and let sleep take me.

15

ALEXA

My cubicle at FLLW is one desk away from the windows, which is better than most of the other marketing assistants have fared. It's purely luck, but I'm new to having luck on my side, so I relish the moments when my office neighbor has vacated his seat and I have an unobstructed view of the Manhattan skyline. It's a gray day, the clouds blanketing the tops of the highest skyscrapers.

I turn back to my computer to finish the agenda for the upcoming meeting with Curt. I've always enjoyed being organized, but this task is one of my least favorites. Christine already seems like the type of person who will always poke a hole or find an error in the agenda.

After I'm done, I make my way around the corner to the printer, then head for the conference room. I see Curt turning the corner with Christine. Locking eyes with me, he gives me a sneaky smile. I have to fight the urge to run and hug him.

We steal glances throughout the meeting. He's next to Christine, so it's easier than when he's next to me. As Christine drones on about conversion, I let my mind drift to a daydream where Curt and I live together and spend our Sunday mornings snuggling lazily over coffee. I've seen people do this in movies, and it's one thing I've always wanted. But with Beth around, it will never happen. I keep asking her for updates on her apartment search, but she either deflects or acts as if I'm the jerk for wanting her out. What is it they say about houseguests—they, like fish, start to smell after three days? We are way past that three-day mark.

By the time I rejoin the present moment, Christine is hammering out a strict timeline for Curt.

"Alexa, will you be able to stay a little late to help him film?" she asks.

"Of course," I say, taking another opportunity to look into his piercing green eyes.

"Great, order dinner for you both and the team too," she directs as she slides the company AMEX over.

The meeting drags on another hour or so, and my mind continues to drift through fantasies of a life with Curt. I've never dreamt of my wedding in great detail before, but I find myself picturing what ours would look like. I see us on a beach somewhere I've never been, but it's the way he looks at me that I fixate on. The feeling that someone chose me. Loves me.

Finally, Christine hammers through the outline again, more to herself than to the team. I look at my phone in my lap and see that it is 6:01. Jesus, a two-hour meeting? I can't decide if Christine is meticulous or just plain inefficient. Or maybe it's a combination. I've never been a super good judge of character, so I suppose it's a good thing that my role won't involve me being put on any hiring committees.

As we stand to leave the room, Christine reminds me to place the dinner order and to meet Curt at the studio on the basement level of the building. I obviously don't mind having to stay late to work on his projects. It gives us more time together, and there is a little added excitement that no one knows our secret.

We file out of the room, me stealing one more look at Curt before I head for my desk. I'm around the corner before I realize I don't know what Curt wants to eat. I look around—most people have gone home for the day, but I opt to text him instead of turning back to ask him. We normally don't ask for orders; we're supposed to just pick something and make sure it shows up. I can't help wanting to make him extra happy.

What do you want for dinner? I text with a smile.

I hear the familiar double chime of my phone as I reach my desk.

Chinese?

My smile grows larger. *You read my mind.*

I hop online and place a massive order for the team to be delivered to the studio. I debate surprising Beth and sending something for her to eat since she's home alone, but I decide she's probably already ordered something. She's never been one to wait on other people. I shut down my computer and pack up, and as I make my way through the empty halls, my mind drifts again to Curt. This time we're not lounging around reading the paper but making love. And it's not Sunday morning; it's night. As I wait for the elevator, a rush of warmth takes over my body. It's an unfamiliar feeling for me, this desire for another. I spent so much of my life wanting to be free of Beth because I felt smothered, and now I want to feel . . . well . . . smothered.

I want Curt. I need him.

Unlike during the daytime hours, the elevator makes a rapid descent without any stops.

The hallway leading to the studio is lined with red lights, making it look like the emergency evacuation route on a plane. They indicate studios in "Recording" and those that are not. When I find Studio 17, I'm relieved to see that the light is off. They must not have begun yet.

Curt is behind the kitchen set, setting up a double boiler. An assistant is carrying over the stand mixer, and I see a bowl with eggs and another with chunks of dark chocolate. Curt must have filmed one episode already, because the German Chocolate Cake Balls segment was scheduled to be done second. I take a seat at one of the open tables in the back and unpack my laptop and notebook. Early on, Christine told me I'd be asked to assist on shoots, but this is my first one, and there must be fifteen other people here. Mitch, one of the other marketing assistants, always complains about shoots. He calls it "bitch work" and warned me how demeaning those days can be.

Mitch has a master's in fine arts from Columbia but no work experience, so his expectations in this current climate are wildly outrageous. Still, I like Mitch, so I pretend to commiserate. But the truth is, I'd wash the floor with a toothbrush to be near Curt.

My phone pings as we're on the third video—vegan stir-fry— alerting me that our not-so-vegan food has arrived. I quietly slink out the door, closing it with precision and patience so I won't make a sound as I leave. My right side twinges. Precision and patience are something I've had to learn.

I meet the delivery man at the front security desk, not surprised to see he's still wearing his bike helmet. I cannot imagine delivering food via bicycle in this city—it seems as if it'd be more like a death sentence than a career move. I take the three massive paper sacks from him and make my way toward the elevator. There's no way I can open the doors to the stairwell with these.

As I approach the studio, I see the light is off, so I enter with less stealth and announce that dinner is here. The director tells everyone to take thirty minutes. I am still setting the plastic trays and boxes out when I realize the entire crew is already lined up. I step back and let them dig in like a herd of wild animals. Mitch also warned me about TV crews and free food. My face must be broadcasting my thoughts because Curt joins me at a safe distance and chuckles. "TV crews love free food, don't they?"

"I'd say so."

His hand brushes mine, and I pull it back, afraid someone will see. When I give him a scolding look, he just winks.

"So, when do we get to be alone again?" he says with a new frankness.

"I don't know."

"Tonight?" he asks.

I sigh, unsure how to tell him about my current roommate. He can't meet Beth. Not yet. Given how she's been behaving lately, maybe not ever.

"I can walk you home after this is over," he says.

There's no avoiding it—I have to tell him about her or else start a complicated series of lies. And I know from experience that lies only multiply.

"Well, it's a little hard because my sister is in town," I say.

"Oh! No worries. Maybe this weekend?"

"Yeah, maybe." I sound wistful.

"What is it?"

"I'm just . . . not sure how long she will be in town. Her situation is a little complicated."

"Why don't we all do something?" he says. "I've been excited to meet her."

There's something about the way he says it. Or maybe it's just *what* he's said, because I don't remember telling him about her. I don't remember telling him I even had a sister. But I brush it off. I did have a lot of wine that night—maybe I did mention Beth.

"How about we go to your place instead?" I suggest.

He laughs. "Well, that's a little complicated too. I have two roommates."

"Roommates are better than sisters."

"Not *my* roommates."

He doesn't know my sister.

When it's clear I'm not going to give on this, he gives a wry smile. "Well, let me walk you home at least."

That I agree to. "Sure," I tell him. "That would be great."

After filming two more videos, the director wraps. It's just before ten o'clock, but the long day has it feeling as though it's much later.

Curt waits until we are a good ten blocks from the office to take my hand. Then we duck under awnings and kiss. We continue to kiss our way downtown, him pressing me against the brick walls and big glass windows. By the time we reach my building, I'm dizzy with desire.

"Can I please come up?" he pants.

We've been kissing outside the door, and it must have melted my resistance, because this time I don't say no. I take my keys from my purse and open the first door.

As we ascend the stairs, however, the fear of my sister looms like a shadow at the back of a crowded amusement park. I open the door slowly and quietly, and we tiptoe through the living room. When I see Beth asleep on the couch, I quickly pull Curt into the bedroom.

"She must be out having some fun of her own, huh?" he says, his lips against my neck.

I don't correct him, instead slowly unbuttoning his shirt. He pulls my top off, and for a moment I forget about my scar—until I feel his hand pause on top of it before continuing to explore the rest of my body.

There's no need to drift into a daydream now. I'm living my fantasy in this present moment with Curt. It doesn't matter that I'm a virgin, or that I never told him I'm a virgin, because soon it no longer matters.

I am no longer a virgin but a woman. A woman in love.

16

BETH

While I've never wanted to live in the city, I do have to appreciate the convenience of things. There truly is a coffee shop, a deli, and a nail salon on every corner in Manhattan. It must be a city ordinance, one that I will never complain about.

The nail salon four storefronts down from Alexa's building is pretty busy. A small Asian woman appears from thin air and greets me before asking, "What you need?" in broken English.

I tell her, "A manicure, please" as I grab a shiny bottle of glitter-black polish from the display rack and show her my nails. Her chuckle at that is offensive, but I suppose I can't blame her. It looks as if I've never had them done before.

She seats me in a white chair at a white lacquered desk. A younger Asian woman named "Heidi" joins me and smiles as she rubs away what's left of my previous polish. Her accent is even thicker, so we don't talk much. She motions to a water bowl, and after I comply with the instruction to soak, she takes one of my hands and begins to file my nails. I hate the feeling, so instinctively I yank my hand back. I know a lot of people who dislike the sensation of their nails being filed. For me, it's the seemingly slow sawing of my nails, and if the rhythm is off at all, it sends a chill all through my body. Who would like that?

She rather forcefully reaches across the desk to take my hand back.

"NO!" I scream.

"It okay," she says, still reaching for my hand.

I push my chair back, shaking my head.

"Just paint," I instruct her.

"I file," she insists.

Another woman joins her, and they begin speaking in a language I cannot understand. Finally, the woman who initially greeted me joins them and tries to explain that my nails need to be filed.

They begin to talk rapidly among each other, all three of them exchanging the occasional laugh, no doubt at my expense.

I cannot take it anymore. This was a terrible idea. I feel the rage building like a bottle of champagne I cannot recork. Standing, I grab my bag and the glass of water they gave me upon my arrival.

"No fucking filing!" I scream, throwing the glass of water against the wall behind the woman. I repeat the words over and over as I throw the chair to the floor next. I'm still screaming as I approach the exit. My finale comes at the cost of the orchid plant sitting on the front desk. With a swoop of my right hand, I send the botanical crashing to the floor.

"Fuck you!" I say as punctuation before yanking open the door. A mess of bells hung over it jangle as I slam it behind me.

Once I'm safely back inside Alexa's apartment, I sit on the sofa and regain my breath and composure. I look down at my hands. They actually look a lot better than before, so it wasn't a total loss.

I reach for the laptop again—time for another escape into Curt's past.

17

ALEXA

It's late when I finally wake up. I don't remember falling asleep after making love to Curt last night, but I must have, because the sun only slants over the bed this way just before noon.

Instinctively, I turn to find Curt, but he's gone. Shocked, I scramble for my phone, then feel immediate relief when I see a message from seven this morning. I check the current time. Eleven. I haven't slept this late in years.

I open his text.

Last night was amazing. I didn't want to wake you. Can I see you again tonight?

I type my response: *It was amazing, and yes, please.*

I watch the three little bubbles and wait for his reply.

Movie?

Sounds perfect! xx

I set the phone back on the nightstand and roll back over. My mind debates just hanging in bed all day, reliving every memory from last night. But then I hear Beth in the other room.

When I open my door, she's sitting on the sofa examining her hands. My laptop is in front of her, screen open. I wish she'd stop using it, or at least put it away when she's done. I try to see what she's been searching, but she always deletes the history.

"That fucking nail salon next door is the worst. Don't go. Ever," she warns with sincerity.

"Oh, you've already been out?"

"Yeah. Big mistake."

I shake my head and join her on the sofa. The TV is set to Bravo. Beth must have been watching it again last night.

"You worked late, huh?" she asks calmly.

Is it possible she didn't hear or see us? She was in that deep of a sleep? I wonder before I reply, "Yeah, super late."

"Look at you, working girl."

"Yep. Real professional over here."

I wait for her to call me out, but she says nothing. She just laughs along to the show.

"I have to run a couple errands. Do you want to come?" I ask.

"No. I've had enough people for today."

"Okay. I'll be back in a couple hours."

"Sounds good."

I walk to the bathroom and start the shower. As I'm lathering, I notice my own nails looking rather bare. I decide that I'll get them done after my other errands.

~

Three hours later, my arms are beginning to cramp from the groceries and dry cleaning I've picked up while out and about the town. Stopping, I readjust my load once more before I turn the corner of my block. As I move the hangers to my left hand, I realize I've forgotten to do something about my bare nails. I normally wouldn't bother, but all the other women at work take care of their nails. I often overhear them talking about what a difference a manicure makes for your confidence—there must be something to that.

Deciding I'll go back out, I struggle through the front door and up the three flights of stairs to my apartment. It's moments like these that I curse this building for not having an elevator. I drop the groceries to the floor, schlep the plastic-covered dry cleaning to my bedroom, and toss it haphazardly on my bed. I'll deal with that later. As I pick the bags up to bring the groceries to the kitchen, I realize Beth isn't here.

The calm is nice, but didn't she say she didn't feel like going out again?

Whatever. I've sacrificed too much of my life to my sister's moods.

After I've put the last bag of groceries away, I run downstairs to the nail salon on our block. I know Beth warned against it, but she's more particular than your average person, and I don't want to trek all over the place to find a salon that may or may not be even worse than this one. Even a crap paint job is worth the convenience.

When I enter the small space, the technicians' heads are bowed, their eyes focused on their work as Taylor Swift drums through the speakers. A small Asian woman emerges from what I assume is the back staff room. She doesn't see me at first, but when she does, she gasps.

No, it's more of a scream.

I turn and look behind me, terrified of what I may find, but there's nothing that should have provoked that. When I turn back, the small woman is up in my face, and she's yelling. I don't understand what is happening.

"You need leave. Get out!" she shouts.

"Me?" I ask. I've never been here. How could I not be allowed to be here?

"You get out now. I call police."

"Why?"

"You broke glass and cause scene. You need to leave."

"I've never been here," I assure her, but she's scooting me with her hands.

"You here earlier. Are you crazy? You a crazy person?"

My hands start to shake at *that* word. And then it all becomes clear. It feels like a bullet to my chest. Beth. No wonder she told me not to come here.

"Whatever she did, it wasn't me, I promise."

I'm about to cry and I don't know why. What has Beth done? People have confused me for my sister before, but never like this. I did nothing wrong, but the hate in her eyes hurts.

The women behind her are speaking in a language I can't understand, while the stunned patrons just watch. The shooing woman's face has changed—she looks confused now too.

"You not here before?" she says.

"No."

I show her my nails, and she squints at me.

"You sure you not here before?"

"No, no, it was my sister. But if you're not comfortable, I can leave."

After a few seconds, she lets out a big sigh.

"No. No. Is okay. Come. Sit."

She takes me by the arm and leads me to a seat, where she hands me a ring of single nails on a silver circle. Each is painted a different color with the number written on the underside. I'm used to just picking from a wall of actual nail polish, or from those revolving stands, like they have for sunglasses. The nail circle is a little creepy, but I pick a red one and pass the circle back to her.

"You want water?"

"No, thank you. I'm fine."

She smiles, and a woman who looks seventeen appears with a bowl of warm water. She soaks my fingers, then takes one of my hands.

"Do you want me to cut or file?"

"Just file, please."

She looks at me oddly and then gives a nervous laugh. After staring at me for a few more odd moments, she proceeds to file my nails into perfectly symmetrical semicircles. After thirty minutes, my nails are dry, and I make my way to the front desk to pay.

"Twenty-three dollah," the owner tells me.

I produce thirty dollars from my wallet and hand it to her. She begins to reach for change, and I immediately stop her. "No, it's okay. That's a tip."

She smiles and tucks the money into the register. "Thank you. Have good day."

I step onto the street and take a deep breath. Whoever said manicures were relaxing doesn't have Beth as a sister.

I need to have a talk with her about behaving like this while she's staying with me. I hate being the responsible one. The one with all the consequences. She acts out, and I always have to clean it up.

I turn the lock and slowly open the door. No TV noises. But her voice floats over from the couch.

"Lex, is that you?"

I turn the corner and see her on the sofa in the living room, the laptop in front of her.

"We need to talk, Lex."

"Yeah. We do."

When she just looks at me strangely, I show her my nails.

"I don't get it," she says.

"I went to the salon downstairs . . ."

Understanding dawns. So does her anger.

"I told them not to file my fucking nails," she spits.

I look at her for any signs of remorse but see nothing. I decide I don't have it in me to lecture her. Plus, I need to conserve my energy for our fights about Curt. And she doesn't know the news yet. I'm not going to tell her now. I'm just going to relax and unwind from the stressful manicure.

"Wanna watch a movie?" she asks as if she's reading my mind.

"Sure. Tell me what you want," I say, picking up the remote.

She picks an old movie. One I haven't seen. I see "Joan Crawford" and "Bette Davis" in big cursive letters cover the screen. Then *Whatever Happened to Baby Jane* takes its place. It seems like a classic old movie, like *Breakfast at Tiffany's*, but I know my sister's taste, and I'll bet this is more twisted than the idyllic home on the screen suggests.

18

BETH

I think we've seen the movie twenty times. I'm not sure why our parents let us watch it so young. It's a bit twisted, but I suppose that must be part of the allure. To be honest, I'm more interested in the real-life drama between Joan Crawford and Bette Davis. I try to picture them in modern day, maybe on Bravo trying to ride out the last potentials of their dying careers.

"You hungry?" I ask Alexa as the credits roll.

"Not really."

"Well, I'm going down to the bodega to get something then."

"Okay."

I grab my wallet and head downstairs. It's brighter than I expect it to be. And louder. The bodega on the corner has great bacon, egg, and cheese bagels. I walk up the two tiny steps and push my body against the door, only to be met with extreme resistance. I step back and see a yellow lined piece of paper with the words WILL RETURN IN 20 MINUTES scribbled in all caps in the middle. Fuck.

I settle on a slice of pizza. There are a few places around here.

Alexa loves Joe's, but I want Bleecker Street. It's a couple blocks away but worth it, and I grab the pizza to go on a paper plate. After enjoying my cheese slice, I decide to cut through the alley as a shortcut. I shove the last piece of crust in my mouth and drop the plate on the ground, but I can hear Alexa's voice yelling "don't litter" in my brain.

I bend down to grab the trash but nearly lose the pizza I just ate as I see what the plate has landed on. It takes me a moment to make sense of what I'm looking at, but these eyes are staring right at me over a mouth agape in horror. It's the head of a small bird, and there's no way it just came off like that on its own. Gross. This city is so fucked up. I drop the plate into the nearest trash bin and shake off the sketchy dead bird.

I'm climbing the stairs when I suddenly realize that Alexa just let me off the hook pretty easily given that I told an entire salon to fuck off. She didn't lecture me or tell me to order in. She let me go back out—risking that I would embarrass her again—without any pause or fight.

What's she up to? I wonder.

Alexa may be the weaker of us, but she doesn't back down from every fight that easily. Especially ones that stem from me embarrassing her.

We've never kept much from each other, which makes it all the more obvious when there's something she's keeping from me. I don't remember how old we were, but it was one of our last beach days before the incident. I remember being at the beach, sitting in the warm sand. We were working diligently on a sandcastle, the kind where you dripped the wet grains into formation, ending up with something more like Gaudí than Michelangelo. Messy but still masterful.

"I want to go catch sand crabs," Alexa announced, stopping

work on her tower of the castle abruptly and pulling me up with her to move closer to the incoming tide.

"I'm not done," I declared and dragged her back down. "I want to finish my castle."

"No," she retorted, pulling me toward the tide again. "Can't we just catch a few and then finish your dumb castle?"

"Be nice, you two," Mom called to us from the deeper sand farther up the beach. She was situated under a yellow-and-white umbrella in one of those folding chairs, a cooler to her left housing all of our snacks. Dad was sitting in a similar chair with his head tilted back. I couldn't hear him from where I sat in the sand, but I knew he was snoring.

"Five minutes, then we're going back to the castle," I told Alexa.

She turned and looked at me, a tiny little crab wiggling around in the wet sand in the palm of her small hand. I could tell she wanted to say something.

"What is it?" I asked.

"What?"

"You look like you're about to say something," I told her. "Something that probably isn't that nice."

She knelt down and dropped the crab. He skittered away, quickly disappearing below the wet sand. Little bubbles peppered the sand all around, and I knew that this meant the crab and his friends were burrowing farther down and awaiting the next wave.

"What is it?" I asked again.

"It's nothing," she huffed. "Let's go finish the castle."

I followed her back to our warm, sandy seats and happily resumed my work on the tower. She was pretty quiet for the rest of the day, and I remember not really caring what it was but knowing that she had kept something from me for the first time. We were young, so I didn't think much of it until the incident. Then I was pretty sure what the look meant that day on the beach.

I'm not sure what she's hiding now, only that she is hiding something. She only lets me get my way that easily when she's preparing for something bigger down the line. This makes my skin prickle a little.

What do you have in store, Lex?

19

ALEXA

I fumble with the awkwardly shaped tube of mascara. I never understood the need to make things pretty until I started working at FLLW. Marketing is fun and creative, but sometimes I find my inner dialogue questioning the ethics behind it, given we outright lie to so many consumers. Of course, I never tell anyone this but Beth, as I know she shares my feelings.

I'm finishing my left eye when I hear the buzzer sound.

"Beth, did you order takeout?" I yell.

"Nope!" she calls back.

I judge from her lackluster response that she isn't expecting anything or anyone. I move toward the buzzer and press the two-way talk button. "Hello?"

"Hey!" Curt's voice calls back.

"What are you doing here?" I snap. "You were supposed to meet me at the theater."

"Are you going to let me up or what?"

Fuck.

"I'll be down in just a second."

I release the button before he can say anything else. When he was here last night, Beth was asleep. But tonight, she's here, she's awake, and I'm not ready for them to meet. I rush back to the bathroom and quickly finish applying mascara. Then I toss the tube in my makeup bag and race for my bedroom.

I grab the first tank I see and a pair of jeans from the laundry pile, then pull my sneakers out from beneath the bed. I'm slipping the shoes on when Beth interrupts.

"I didn't know he was coming here. Can I meet him?"

"No, we're going to be late."

I look up and see her standing in the doorway. Her face is softer than normal, showing signs of her disappointment.

"Soon," I say. "Promise."

I give her a hug, grab my bag, and sprint out the door and down the stairs. Curt's sitting on the steps leading up to the building's door.

"Hey! Sorry to keep you waiting," I tell him, searching his face for some clue as to why he's just shown up here.

"Yeah, but I like picking you up."

I smile and take his hand as we walk to the theater.

After the movie, I'm in a daze. Curt's selection has left me in a foggy hell. It was gory and sick, and I felt tense the whole time. Once we step back out into the night, which is surprisingly cool for July, I'm exhausted.

"I'm not sure you should come up," I say as we reach my building's door. "Beth."

He leans in and kisses me. "It's okay. I understand."

I lose myself and my worries in Curt, and I fumble with the keys to let us in. We take our time making our way up. As I open the door, I say a silent prayer that Beth's either out or asleep.

I don't see her. Rather than test my luck, I lead him into my bedroom and quickly close the door.

Hours later—or at least I presume it is hours later, given the morning light seeping through the window—I'm awoken by a touch on my side.

Curt. Curt is touching my scar.

I instinctively push his hand away and cover myself in the blankets.

"What happened?" he asks softly.

I take a deep breath and come back to my surroundings. He's safe. I'm safe.

"It's a long story," I murmur. "Do you want coffee?"

"Sure!"

"Milk? Sugar?"

"Yes and yes."

I lean over and kiss him as I'm tying my robe around my body. "Be right back."

Beth is sleeping on the sofa, her back to me. I place a pod in the Keurig machine on the counter and remove two mugs from the cabinet. I think about grabbing a third for Beth, but I never know what she is or isn't eating and drinking. And who knows when she went to bed, or how long she will sleep.

As the first cup finishes, I replace the pod with another and swap the full mug for my empty one. While the second cup brews, I open the refrigerator and reach for the almond milk I keep on the top shelf. That's when I see it.

A scream rips from me faster than I can control. Even though I stifle it halfway through, Curt calls out to ask if I'm okay.

"Yes, fine, just a spill. Be right there," I assure him as I steady myself. My body shakes as I gather what feels like hundreds of paper towels in my hand. Squeezing my eyes shut, I reach in and remove the small decapitated bird from the refrigerator shelf. Then I place the carcass in the garbage and cover it with the mass of towels.

I wipe the blood from the shelf of the refrigerator with more paper towels before washing my face and hands furiously. Afterward, they're almost raw, the way my hands were for all of 2020 during the pandemic. I stop and finish making the coffees.

Throughout it all, Beth sleeps on the couch.

I'm furious. Madder than I've been in years.

Before I reenter my room, I make sure to relax my face. I hand him the mug, then circle around to the other side of the bed and climb back in.

"Sounds like it was a lot of work! Thank you!"

"No, the spill just startled me. Not quite awake yet, I guess." I smile and set my mug down to free my hands and body to snuggle with him. I lie with my head on his chest and try to relive last night, but just like the horror film, my happy images are suddenly slashed in half, with images of the decapitated bird forcing their way through. I listen to his slow heartbeat to try to steady mine.

20

BETH

I'm almost falling back asleep when I hear Alexa walk past me into the kitchen. I keep my back facing the sofa, hoping Curt leaves soon.

I need to talk to my sister about what I found online about him last night. I didn't want to confront them both, because he actually scares me a little.

I'm lying there, going over my plan to tell Alexa, when her scream interrupts my thoughts. My instinct is to get up and run to her, to protect her, but my body doesn't move. I hear Curt call to her, "Are you okay?" and she quickly responds back with "Yes, fine, just a spill. Be right there."

I know my sister didn't scream from a spill; it takes much, much more to make her scream like that. She covered it well enough to convince Curt. But he doesn't know my sister, and I don't want him to.

I wake to find Alexa looming over me. She's still in her robe.

"What the fuck, Beth?"

I look at her, unable to respond. I'm still a bit drowsy, not to mention that I was prepared to be the one delivering bombs, not vice versa.

"Why did you do that with the bird?"

"What bird?"

"Oh, come on, Beth."

I'm genuinely confused. My face must make this clear, because she takes a step back and sits on the floor across from me.

"What are you talking about, Lex?" I say gently.

"The fucking decapitated bird in the refrigerator."

"What? You're kidding."

"Well, it's in the trash now."

She gestures toward the kitchen as if inviting me to go look. I'm admittedly a little curious, so I go to the kitchen and open the lid to the trash, moving the wad of paper towels until I see traces of red. I slowly move another paper towel out of the way, and the small decapitated bird's body knocks the wind from my lungs.

I'm sucked back to the day in our family's den. We liked to do our homework there because there was more space to work. Plus, there was a big window, much larger than the small rectangle in our bedroom, and it meant we could zone out and stare at the street outside to break up the monotony of fractions and ancient history.

On that day, I was staring out the window, but Lex was still working on her homework when our mom screamed. Alexa was the first to race toward our room, and I almost ran into her when she stopped abruptly at the door. It was only when I peeked my head over her shoulder that I saw our mom hunched over something, sobbing.

"Mom?" Alexa said.

Mom looked up, and I saw she was holding Susan, our family

cat. Alexa began to cry. Susan wasn't moving. I racked my brain for answers but came up empty.

"Why did you do this?" Mom said, staring at Alexa.

"Mom, it wasn't me," she insisted.

I was still confused, trying to figure out why Mom thought Alexa killed Susan. Then I saw it. The rope around Susan's neck.

I had told Mom and Dad at least a dozen times that I had some allergy to Susan—it was driving me nuts. I even asked Alexa to try to convince them to give her away so that I could stop sneezing. I felt as if they were ignoring me. I didn't mean to . . . well, I didn't plan to. I just snapped. I'd had enough. I wanted some kind of relief. Or maybe I wanted some kind of reaction—nobody seemed to care, and I had to take matters into my own hands.

Suddenly nauseated, I ran to the bathroom and retched in the toilet. After several minutes, I pulled myself up and splashed water on my face. I was walking back toward the room when I heard them.

"Mom, it was Beth. It wasn't me."

"Alexa, stop."

"Mom, I swear." She was sobbing now.

"That's it. You're going to a facility. You need help, more than what Dad and I can give you."

Mom left the room and disappeared down the hall, Susan's lifeless tail swaying slightly in her arms.

When she was gone, Alexa still sobbed. She was in the fetal position, clutching her side.

"Lex?"

Sitting up, she glared at me with what can only be described as hate.

"Why did you do it?" she screamed. "Look what you've done."

"I didn't," I began, but she cut me off.

"I hate you," she said. "Just go away. I hate you."

That was when I realized Mom was standing in the doorway, her face as horrified as if she'd just seen a ghost. After she ran into the den, I waited a few moments and then followed her. She was sitting at the computer, Googling something.

The next day Alexa went to the Weinstein Center for the first time.

I snap back to the present moment and feel the same pit in my stomach. Alexa blamed me for a lot when we were younger, but she stopped when she started seeing Dr. Greer. This is the first time in a long time that she doesn't believe me.

"It wasn't me," I tell her softly. "But there is something I need to tell you. It's about Curt."

"Of course it is." She turns away. "I don't want to know."

"Alexa, listen. I don't think he's who he says he is."

"It's pretty hard to steal an identity when you're internet famous, Beth," she snarks. She sounds very LA Gen Z now when she talks about work.

"That's not what I mean. I found some stuff. He's got a dark past, Lex."

"Don't we all?"

Her comment hits me like a punch to the chest, so I fire back. "Maybe *he* did that with the bird. He's been to rehab. He has priors, has been arrested for shoplifting. And other things."

"So? That's no worse than what I've done, is it?"

"Alexa, he has two arrests for stalking."

"Beth, stop! I love him. And he loves me."

Her words hit me like a bullet.

"Love?" I shout. How on earth could these two be in love already? The notion is beyond ridiculous.

"*Yes*. He loves me. The real me. So I don't care about his past."

I feel the fear rising. "What do you mean, the *real* you? What have you told him?"

"Nothing. But he wouldn't care. He's not like that."

"Oh god, Alexa, you're playing with fire. Do you want to go back into a facility? Do you want to give up your freedom? Give up your life? Your work?" I ask, but she just stares at me silently. Then I finally ask the hardest question. "You'd give me up? For him?"

"No. I'm not going back anywhere *or* giving anything up. He's not like that. He won't care." She doesn't answer the last question.

"You can't tell him. You can't."

"He wants to meet you."

I have watched a few of those UFC fights. They're bloody but impressive. Every once in a while, one guy or gal will make such perfect contact with the other's head that you can almost hear their brain blacking out through the television screen.

Her words hit me just like that. And like the fighters, I black out.

21

ALEXA

"And don't forget to hit that subscribe button below so you never miss a new recipe. Thanks for hanging out—I'm Curt Kempton."

A director yells, "Cut!" immediately after Curt stops speaking. When he announces we have what we need now, I watch the crew's energy shift as they sense freedom at the end of the tunnel. It's getting late, and none of them want to be here, filming YouTube promotional videos. I'm probably the only one who doesn't mind.

I begin to pack up my computer and notepad. I wasn't actually using them much, but I didn't want to be the obvious fangirl, staring at my boyfriend with drool dripping down my chin. I'm almost packed up when I realize we're the last two in the studio.

"You killed it," I say.

"You think? I feel like I could have mentioned Phat Food more?"

"No, it's perfect. They'll add the logo to the video in post-production," I assure him.

"God, I love you," he says, pulling me in for a kiss before I have a chance to respond or to process what he's just said. I let my body tell him I feel the same way. Finally, I pull back and smile.

"You love me?" I ask.

"Duh! I've been wanting to tell you."

"I love you too!" I shout, quickly scanning the room to make sure we're still the only ones here.

"Can I walk you home?" he asks.

"Duh!" I say with a smile before slowly pulling him in for one more kiss.

We make our way through the empty halls, waving to Ernesto, the newest security officer, on the way out.

"*Hasta mañana!*" Curt says.

Ernesto nods, and I don't have the heart to tell him that Ernesto is Brazilian. I just smile sympathetically.

We stroll along our normal route, walking, talking, and kissing. But when we're only a few blocks from my building, Curt's energy starts to change. He even drops my hand.

"You okay?" I ask.

"Yeah, I'm just stressed. You're lucky you have your own place."

"What do you mean?"

"Well, Tim and Steve, my roommates . . . well, last night they told me they were in love."

"Both of them? With who?" I ask, not entirely sure why this is such a disaster.

"With each other!" he says. "I mean, great for them, but they want me to move out."

"Oh!" I say, still unsure how to react. "Why?"

"They want to have a spare room for guests and turn my room into a gym. So I'm homeless starting August first."

"Oh, wow, that's soon!" I finally react with a genuine appropriate response. Then a stray thought escapes me. "A gym?"

"Yeah, turns out Tim's ex was loaded, and he just gave him a ton of money to keep quiet, if you know what I mean, so they're going for it."

"Wow. I'm so sorry."

"Yeah, I don't know what I'm going to do."

His eyes are searching mine for a response. I hear the words leave my mouth before I can control them. "You can stay with me," I blurt, then panic. He can't stay with me. Beth is there.

But he's already taking me in his arms and kissing me. "Really? That would be amazing! I love you," he whispers in my ear.

"I love you too," I tell him, and then he pulls away enough for us to start walking again. As we approach my stoop, I reach for my keys but then find myself staring at the lock. He loves me. If he loves me, he'll love Beth. Or at least he'll be able to get along with her, I rationalize.

"Want to celebrate by watching a movie?" he asks.

"Sure." I hesitate. "But are you sure you're ready to meet Beth?"

"Sure! Is she home?"

I hadn't thought about that. I suppose she could be out. She's been harder for me to read lately and even more spontaneous with her plans. "I think so."

Every step through the lobby is one step closer to what may be the biggest meeting of my life. But when we reach the third-floor landing, I get a feeling she isn't home. I unlock the insane number of bolts that adorn all New Yorkers' doors, and Curt follows me inside. The lights are out and the apartment is silent.

There's no sign of Beth in the living room. The sheet set and blanket have been folded haphazardly on the floor.

"She must be out," I tell him.

Curt flops down onto the sofa as if it's already his, and I set my bag on the counter before joining him. I hand him the remote, and he navigates through Netflix with ease.

"Scary? Funny?" he asks.

"Comedy!" I shout, a little desperate after our last movie foray.

I watch him flip through what feels like thousands of movies, willing him to pick one rather than let the trailers blare for thirty seconds and then move on.

"*Wedding Crashers*?" he asks.

I love that movie, but I've seen it so many times.

"Perfect."

"I'm going to use the pisser first." He leaps up and walks to the bathroom. As I hear the door shut and lock, I see Beth standing in the mouth of the hallway. She's wearing my clothes again. And it looks like she's been sleeping. I guess that is happening in my bed now, when I'm not here.

"Hey," she says, her eyes on the shoes Curt's kicked off by the couch.

"Hey, so Curt's here," I tell her.

"Oh. Shit." She looks around as if he might be lying in wait, ready to spring out and attack her.

"He's in the bathroom. Sit," I direct her, and she does, on the lone chair next to the end of the sofa. I hear the toilet flush, then the door creak. *He didn't wash his hands?* I think to myself. I thought everyone knew the importance of hand washing—and all hygiene—after going through the hell that was 2020. But the thought is cut short when Curt reappears. He flops back onto the sofa and puts his arm around me, eyes on the TV, as if he hasn't noticed the other person now in the room.

This is not off to a good start.

"Curt, this is Beth," I tell him gently.

His eyes dart to me, and then when I nod my head to the chair, his gaze follows. After taking his arm away from my shoulders, he straightens up and smiles.

"Hey! I'm so excited to meet you," he says with genuine enthusiasm.

"Yeah, it's good to meet you. I've heard so much about you," she replies.

He shoots me a deer-in-headlights look, as if waiting for me to fill in the blank on what he should say next. When I don't, he sighs.

"So, were you, uh, out?" he asks.

Please be nice, please be nice, please don't mess this up, I will her in my mind.

"Yep. Just out and about. What are you kids up to?"

"We were just about to watch a movie," I say. "Wanna join?"

"Nah, you kids have fun. Lex, mind if I chill in your room?" she asks.

"Of course not. Go ahead," I tell her. I watch as she gets up and walks into the bedroom, then I look back at Curt, who's scratching his head and then patting his hair back in place.

"She, uh, seems cool."

I breathe a sigh of relief and lie back into the sofa. Curt hits play and then wraps his arm back around me. He laughs at the opening scene, and I smile too, but my smile has nothing to do with Owen Wilson and Vince Vaughn. I'm smiling because Curt just met Beth and it went okay. No, it went great.

It was uneventful. And that's all I've ever wanted from my sister—for her to blend in.

22

BETH

This sofa is getting to me. It's not just the overly firm cushions, clearly not chosen with houseguests in mind—it's the haphazardness of the bedding. Curt and Alexa stayed up so late, laughing and giggling at the movie, that I wasn't able to reclaim the living room until what could only be considered the early morning rather than late night. I rotate my neck from left to right, willing it to pop and relieve the pressure mounting in my shoulders. But nothing happens.

Alexa's door is still closed, so I assume they're still in there. I check the clock—only six thirty. They'll be up soon.

I lie back and recall the brief interaction with Curt. I didn't like the way he looked at me. It was creepy, as if he was playacting rather than being introduced to the most important person in his girlfriend's life.

Loud footsteps alert me that they're up—or rather he is. I quickly turn my back to the room and pretend I'm asleep. I don't want to deal with him right now. Last night's meeting was enough. Thankfully, he leaves quickly after gathering the things he's left strewn around the apartment. Once the front door shuts, I turn back and see Alexa in the doorway.

"Hey. You're up," she says with a rare giddy smile.

"Yeah. Curt walks like he's got cinder blocks on his feet."

"Not everyone can be as quiet as you," she says dismissively. "Coffee?"

"No. Thanks."

I think she's going to get up and head to the kitchen, but instead she curls up beside me on the sofa. She's in such a sweet mood. When she lays her head in my lap, I run my hands through her hair, like I did when she was in the hospital. I have always hated being touched, but Alexa finds it soothing.

"I need to tell you something, and you can't freak out, okay?" she says, her smile slowly dimming.

"Jesus, what now?"

"Curt is about to be homeless, so I told him he can move in here for a bit."

"What?"

She sits up as if to better deliver another blow. "His roommates fell in love, and they're kicking him out."

"What?"

"They fell in love with each other, and—anyway, it doesn't matter. He needs a place to stay, and last night he told me he loved me." Her smile returns as she shares the last bit of information.

"Alexa, you don't even know him! And he doesn't know you. How the fuck can you love each other?"

"We do. Trust me. It's real."

"It's not real. It's *insane*."

This time, I use the word deliberately, watching as it hits her like an anvil to the chest. She's done. She's shutting down. I backpedal.

"*You* are not insane—the idea of loving someone after a couple of weeks is insane," I try, but I can tell she's tuned out. Clearly affronted, she heads to her room but turns at the door.

"He's moving in. If you don't like it, maybe you should be the one to leave."

Ouch. Alexa has always wanted to be separate from me. Being a twin is complicated, but it's most painful when two twins want different things. It's a push-pull, one that has quite literally torn us apart in the past.

I lie back and try to sort out the information. I have two priorities. The first is to keep our secrets safe. The second is to keep Alexa safe. And right now, Curt is threatening both of those.

The only thing I know for certain at this point is that I'm not going anywhere, and that I need a plan.

23

ALEXA

Dr. Greer isn't wearing a tie today. Instead, he has on a gray sweater-vest over a short-sleeved white button-up shirt. It must be ninety degrees outside, so his sweater-vest stands out. It's Friday, but I have seen Dr. Greer on many Fridays, and he always has on a tie.

"No tie today?"

"No," he says with a chuckle but no further explanation.

I take my normal seat across from him. We both avoid the sofa. He's the doctor, so I assume he's never sat on it, and I refuse because it's only the craziest of the crazies who actually choose the sofa when they talk to the shrink.

In truth, I've never thought of Dr. Greer as one. Sure, I call him Dr. Greer, but it's the same as calling a teacher Mrs. Hobbs. It's part of the job title. I don't think I'm crazy; I've just had an abnormal life. Being a twin isn't the same as having a sibling. The both of you came from the same egg. You shared the same womb, and you made your entry into the world together. You are joined by a unique bond that exceeds emotion and the mind. It's physical.

"How have you been?" he asks.

"Good," I say, and I mean it.

He smiles. "Good."

"Well, actually, something big has happened."

Here's where I should admit that I don't share everything with Dr. Greer. I don't share everything with anyone, except Beth. I haven't told him that she's been staying with me.

"Curt is going to move in for a little while," I confess. I've talked about Curt in these sessions, but I haven't mentioned that it's the same Curt who worked here in the kitchen until last week—his views are up, and he got a big liquor sponsor. Booze brands have deep pockets, and it turns out crappy wine is great for cooking. We pour him something better when he has to drink it in his videos. But at least he was able to quit his crappy job at Weinstein.

"Wow."

Dr. Greer's never been very wordy. Sometimes we sit in silence as he patiently waits for me to share or confess. But today I feel compelled to explain the decision and to hopefully hear his blessing. Not that it matters, but after Beth's reaction, I just want the support of someone who gets it.

"His roommates fell in love," I start. "With each other." I have learned I need to add that part in when I tell people, because it makes it clearer why they want the place to themselves. "So they're turning the place into their dream apartment, and Curt needs to find a new one."

"I see."

"You know how rent is in this city. And he's an entrepreneur, so he needs to be able to put as much of his earnings as possible back into his brand." I surprise myself with how much of a marketing guru I've become so quickly. "It's just for a little while until he sorts stuff out."

"It's soon, Alexa."

"We love each other."

"I see. What do you love about him?"

"Everything."

"Can you tell me more specifically the things you love?"

I pause. So does Dr. Greer. There are so many things I could say. I love that he loves me. I love that he accepts me. I love that he picked me. I love that he accepts Beth.

"He's kind. Smart. Driven. And I love that he loves and accepts me."

"Accepts you? What do you mean by that?"

"I've been able to open up to him. I feel like he doesn't judge me."

"Judge you for what?"

"My flaws. My past."

"What about your past?"

He's pressing me more than he has in years, and it's making me uncomfortable. I wish Beth were here to say something sassy that would force him to back off. But she isn't. So instead, I shut down. I feel myself pulling inward. Closing down. He must notice it too, because he moves his pen to the yellow legal pad in his lap and begins to write.

"People talk about love at first sight all the time," I blurt.

He stops writing and looks at me.

"They *do*. I've heard many old people say they knew they wanted to marry their wife the day they met her, and fifty years later they're still happy."

"That's true," he says slowly.

"That's what this is."

"It may be. But as your doctor, Alexa, I have to give you all the information. You have a history of instability." He searches my face, trying to gauge my comprehension. "You are aware of this, yes? It's something I ask you to continue to think about from time to time, in particular when you are making your choices."

I nod, but inside I'm not so sure. Am I unstable? Have I been? I don't know. Everyone seems to think so. Everyone except Curt. And Beth.

"So we just want to make sure you take things slowly and make very sound decisions. And moving in with someone is a big decision," he explains. "In fact, loving someone is a big decision. And moving to the city and living alone for the first time was a huge change for you already."

"Loving Curt is not a decision. It's just a fact!"

He looks at me over his glasses. "The emotion may be, but trust me—it's a decision."

"I didn't get to decide if I loved Beth or not. I just did." The words feel like vomit coming out of me. Painful, but afterward I feel a sense of relief.

"You don't have to love Beth," he says.

"She's my sister. She's my twin. She's part of me."

"Love is complicated, but I assure you, it's a choice."

"Agree to disagree." I hurl the words he's used for years against me back at him. It's a final whistle or that proverbial fat lady singing. We are done for today. Or rather, I am done for today. It feels good to make *that* decision.

"Agree to disagree, indeed. Good work today, Alexa. I'll see you next week."

And with that, he ushers me out of his office and into the black-and-white checkerboard halls. I'm in a fog, and it's not until I feel the fading sunlight on my face that I realize I've walked halfway to the subway and don't even remember it. I can't even remember walking out through the Weinstein Center doors. Maybe these sessions aren't so great for me anymore. Maybe I don't need them. As I descend to the underground, his words reverberate in my mind.

Love is a choice.

No, it's not.

I must have said my last thought out loud, because a homeless woman shouts, "Hell yeah, it is!" as I pass by. I glare at her and the small dog by her knee.

My brain swirls, but I keep coming back to the same truth: I love Curt and he loves me. It's the mantra that settles me during my commute home. I don't let my mind worry about Beth yet. Instead, I zone in on the man standing three feet away from me on the platform. He has a large silver chain around his neck. A bike chain. When the doors open, I follow him into the car. It isn't until I'm seated with him across from me that I see what is attached to the chain.

It's a terrarium, about the size of a shoebox. And inside is the largest tarantula I've ever seen. Actually, the only one I've ever seen, at least in person. I shudder, then smile.

New York City can eat you alive, but it's also magical. You never know what the day will bring.

Today, I'm grateful for this man and his tarantula. He's reminded me that maybe I'm really not the crazy one.

24

ALEXA

"Will you grab the milk, please?" I ask Beth the next morning. "I forgot to add some."

She's reading the ad Curt left open on the counter and ignores me.

With a sigh, I go to the kitchen and grab the fridge handle. The refrigerator still gives me chills, since Beth has yet to confess to the whole bird incident. Finding the carton, I pour a splash into Curt's mug and then a bunch in mine. Today, mine says "Life begins at the end of your comfort zone" down the center in white font. The mug was a gift from Dr. Greer one Christmas. We don't exchange gifts anymore, but when I first started seeing him, he'd give me a Christmas gift each year. The mug was the last one. It wasn't until last year that I saw that the quote was not from Ralph Waldo Emerson but from Neale Donald Walsch. Turns out he wrote a book where he asked God questions and then God answered. People criticized him for misrepresenting a book as a conversation with God when it's clearly a conversation he had with himself. But it's still my favorite mug because it's the largest, and I've always needed room for milk and sugar with my coffee.

I carry my mug, along with a normal white mug, to Curt in the living room. I hear Beth following behind. We all squeeze onto the sofa, and Curt turns on the TV.

"Lazy Saturday movie marathon?" he asks us.

"Sure," Beth agrees.

"Sounds perfect!" I add, hoping to cover Beth's lack of enthusiasm. We've been living in this new normal for a couple of days, and so far, if I'm being generous, I'd say we were definitely coexisting.

At least right now my two roommates are quiet, both staring at the screen. I watch Curt scroll through the Netflix options. This tends to be a lengthy process, so I decide to go get my phone from my room. I couldn't care less what we watch—I'm just thrilled they're playing nice.

I grab the phone from my nightstand and see four missed calls from Christine. It's ten on a Saturday morning—what on earth could she want? I hit the call back button and wait for it to ring, but Christine picks up immediately. "Oh, thank God!"

"Christine?"

"Yes, Jesus, fuck . . . hang on."

There's a loud whooshing sound on the other end of the line, followed by a series of crashes. Christine is shouting orders at someone, but those orders are "No, just the tequila, soda, and lime." That's when I realize the crashes are waves and Christine is on vacation in the Bahamas.

"Sorry. Alexa, you there?"

"Yes, is everything okay?"

"No, I swear this happens every time I try to take a vacation.

Listen, some intern fucked up and forgot to leave the Dua Lipa tickets for Marcy, and the show is tonight."

Marcy is one of our biggest clients. Well, she's an agent we have a relationship with; therefore, she brings us a lot of her biggest clients. I wasn't on this particular project, but apparently one of her *Bachelor* contestants-turned-influencers is in town and was scheduled to go to the concert. Christine arranged to get her tickets, but the intern never dropped them at the influencer's hotel.

"So I need you to go to the office and get the tickets. The intern says they're still in my top desk drawer. I swear I'd fire her, but she's just here for college credit. Anyway, can you go now? Like, ASAP?"

"Yeah, of course. But where am I taking them?"

"Oh, she's at the Bowery."

"Okay." I run a mental map of my morning route and start to feel the panic. To go from my apartment to midtown and then across to the Lower East Side and back to the West Village will probably take me at least an hour and a half. I can't leave Curt and Beth alone that long.

"Thank you, babe. Text me as soon as you drop them off."

"Of course. And, hey, Christine?"

"Yeah?"

"Where or who do I leave them with when I get to the Bowery?"

"Oh, leave them at the front desk for Kaitlyn Bristowe. The concierge will handle it."

I recognize the name. It was the one season of *The Bachelor* that I watched. She's a spunky Canadian who's turned her time seeking a husband into an all-out brand. "Okay, I'll leave now."

"Thank you, babe!"

"No problem. Try to enjoy your vacation."

"Ugh. I'll try."

We hang up, and I quickly throw on a loose T-shirt dress and slide into a pair of sneakers. As I run the brush through my hair, I debate what to do with Curt and Beth.

"Do you guys want to come with me to run a quick office errand?" I ask hopefully.

"I'm good," Beth replies first, suppressing a yawn.

"Working on a Saturday, huh?" Curt chides.

I watch him seemingly mull over the idea of joining me before he finally replies, "I think I'll hang with Beth instead."

Crap. I'm not comfortable leaving them alone—well, leaving Curt with Beth. Who knows what trouble she could stir up? But I decide the best thing is just to hurry and hope for the best.

"Are you sure you're comfortable if I leave for an hour or so?"

He looks at Beth, and she shrugs before offering me a smile.

"We'll be fine," she says.

He makes a show of turning his head to my sister. "Hey, have you seen *The OA*?" he asks.

"No. What is it?"

"I've heard it's badass. Mind if we start it, Alexa?" he asks.

"No, go for it. I'll be back soon."

I watch them, and like a mother leaving her young for the first time, I feel equal parts fear and sadness. I'm sad to leave them and terrified of what may happen while they're out from under my supervision.

25

BETH

When Alexa leaves, I sit as far from Curt on the sofa as possible, as if there's an invisible fence around him repelling me. Or maybe I'm the one with the repellent. Either way, I don't want to touch him.

He picked some weird show called *The OA* on Netflix. So far, I'm confused but interested. When I turn to see how he's liking it, he's staring at me with his mouth open like a toddler at a Chuck E. Cheese show.

When the first episode finishes, Curt grabs the remote. "Should we watch the next one?"

"Sure," I say indifferently, but it's actually pretty good. The main character has a lot of secrets, like me—and, I'm starting to think, also like Curt.

The second episode is about to start when I decide to ask Curt more about his past.

"Why did you stalk those girls?" I blurt out. Alexa's always been better at graceful delivery of hard topics, but oh well.

He hits pause, back to looking at me as if I'm a person in a mouse costume.

"I did some research," I confess.

"Oh." He takes a deep breath and sets down the remote. Then he scoots back against the arm of the sofa and faces me. "What do you want to know?"

"I saw that you went to rehab, have been arrested for shoplifting and stalking."

"Yeah. And a couple other minor things, but that's most of it." He hangs his head a moment before lifting it back up. "Gotta love the internet, huh?" he says with a rueful smile.

"I won't let you hurt my sister," I tell him bluntly.

"I'd never hurt your sister. She's more likely to hurt me."

I suddenly worry that she's told him more than I thought.

"Look, we all have a past, and I'm not proud of mine," he explains. "I'm ashamed of my behavior. I was young and stupid."

I stay quiet and wait for him to reveal more.

"I thought I was in love, and I wasn't ready to let the love go," he says.

I swivel my body so I can face him fully. "What if Alexa dumps you? Are you going to stalk her?"

"She won't dump me," he says quickly. "But no, I won't stalk her."

"What about the rehab?"

"It's rehab. Everyone should go." His face is serious. "I mean, aren't we all fighting some interior battle?"

The thought triggers something inside me. Despite how much I don't like this guy, I feel my body and my heart start to soften, the steel walls slowly lowering an inch.

Interior battle.

"One thing I've learned from rehab, jail, and then working at Weinstein," he says, "is that *everyone* is fucked up." I must have nodded or given some clue that I agree, because he continues. "Even

Dr. Greer. No one knows what they're doing—we're all just doing our best to survive."

It's true that I've often questioned Dr. Greer's methods, most notably that he has worked hard to convince my sister that she's crazy. I dislike anyone who tries to drive us apart.

"I've never liked him," he admits.

"You've met him?" I ask, surprised.

"Once. A long time ago. I hate that she still sees him every week." When it's clear that startles me, he adds, "I don't know him well, but since I've been seeing Alexa, she's told me some stuff, and I don't think he's giving her the best advice. I'm not sure he really understands her."

"He absolutely doesn't!" I crow.

As we've been talking, Curt's leaned in closer, and I notice my body language has changed too. I force myself to sit back and regain my composure. Curt follows suit. After a moment he picks up the remote.

"Back to the show?" he suggests.

I nod. As the show resumes, I wonder what just happened. It's hard to focus on the screen, so I mostly dart looks at Curt. He's watching the show, mouth slightly parted. Have I been wrong about him? It doesn't happen often. Still, an ally against Dr. Greer and the Weinstein Center is a win for me. I decide to ease up on the Curt sabotage mission and restrategize. How can we get her away from the doctors?

A brief fantasy pops into my mind, then. The three of us, living in harmony. Peacefully. Happily.

26

ALEXA

The next Friday morning Christine is back from her vacation. We have a meeting scheduled in the largest and most chic conference room, Christine's favorite. My favorite is the small one a few floors down, which is entirely painted purple, like an homage to Prince.

"Alexa, walk with me," I hear Christine say from above my desk. I immediately grab my notebook and stand to follow.

"What happened with the tickets for Kaitlyn Bristowe?"

My heart stops.

"What do you mean?" I immediately respond.

"Marcy called and said Kaitlyn never got the tickets."

She's angry.

"I dropped them off at the Bowery," I manage. "That's where you said, right?"

"Well, she checked with the desk, and they never got them."

Shit. I pause, searching my brain for any possible response. But I'm stunned when Christine beats me to it.

"I always tell clients to never leave tickets or anything at a front desk. Those grimy little shits always steal and blame it on us."

A wave of relief calms the pulsing nerves in every part of my body.

"Plus, I guess Kaitlyn had a better option that night and was going to give them away to a fan or something. Crisis averted," she chirps with a smile.

We enter the conference room, and I see we are the last ones to arrive.

"Charlie, can you hand everyone the numbers?" Christine asks before she's even taken her seat.

The newest and youngest assistant stands and passes out the packets.

"Okay, if you look at the first page, you can see that your engagement factors have gone up," Christine begins, then pauses before adding, "which is great!"

Even though her voice is chipper, I wait for what I know is coming. Curt knows it too. It's not hard to know when your numbers aren't where they should be. Missing a couple of zeros is obvious. I know Curt; he wants over one million followers, and he's still down around thirty thousand.

"When we started working on your business, we obviously set high goals, and the bottom line is we'd like to see these numbers higher," she states to a round of collective nods.

"What do I need to do?" Curt asks.

"As you know, Instagram, YouTube, and Facebook are always changing their algorithm, and we are doing our best to keep on top of what they want. There are even rumors that engagement numbers will go away completely."

"Well, not completely," I interject. "The metrics will be visible to the creator and anyone with access on the back end. Just not to the followers."

"Right. But we don't know the effect it will have on the platforms overall," she says.

I hear the sharpness around the word "effect" and resist the urge to further correct my boss. The truth is, living on my own and now with Curt has given me a new self-confidence. I used to rely on Beth for that, but now I know I'm good at both my job and being Curt's girlfriend.

When I tune back in, Christine is winding up.

"Let's all go home this weekend and come up with our best plans to break through. Something viral," Christine says before quickly adding, "but authentic, of course."

After the meeting adjourns, I head straight for my desk. Since Curt is living with me now, I'm less compelled to sneak around the office with him. Plus, I want to help him reach his goals. If he needs something viral, I want to come up with the best plan.

At my desk, I watch as the sun dips, giving way to the weekend. I'm on a reddit thread to see if there are any new leaks about what the platforms are secretly promoting. If I can figure that out, then Curt's videos have a better shot of being naturally promoted. It's a giant puzzle, where the pieces shift every day. I watched a movie once on the guy that invented the computer, Alan Turing. He and his team were trying to decode the Nazi communication machine, Enigma. Every day they had twenty-four hours to break the code, and every night, at midnight, the Nazis reset it. Social media work is kind of like this—minus the whole world-war-and-genocide aspect, obviously.

I read a particularly interesting thread from @MarkkkkkEEEmarccc that shares his supposed insider info:

> I have a friend who works for a particular social platform, and turns out they're really bummed

that it's turned into such fake and curated content. They want it to go back to random, in-the-moment posts. I doubt any of these influencers will have the balls to have an ugly feed, but that's the scoop, yo.

It's hard to believe that anyone would want to give up Facetune and professional photographers and go back to Nashville and Valencia. But my instinct tells me it's worth a shot. We can spend the weekend tweaking it.

My plan is to create seven nonproduced episodes a week. I envision a home cell video of what he's making or eating that day. A quick edit and upload will not only stand out for the lack of production value but subtly suggest meal-planning and recipes for his followers in real time. The constant content will appeal to a larger audience and, therefore, should spike his numbers. I'm relying on the information from @MarkkkkkEEEmarccc for the final blow. If this is what they want, then it should land in the top videos and gain organic promotion. And usually where there's organic promotion, soon after comes the trend piece, where the early adopters are featured and go viral.

Voilà.

On the train home, I reflect back on the last week. Things have been joyfully uneventful. Beth has been rather independent—unusual, and who knows where she goes—but when she is around, she's pleasant to Curt. I hope when she's out, she's apartment hunting. I don't know how long I can handle our current arrangement. Curt and I have made love every day. I never knew that was something I could have. Plus, Christine complimented me on another campaign idea this morning. And without outright saying why, they moved my cubicle over to the window. I think it's because they are impressed with my work—aside from needing to boost Curt's progress, my other projects are all on track.

I'm lost in my happy life when the train stops abruptly inside the tunnel. I've heard of this, but it hasn't happened to me yet.

When a voice comes over the speaker and says, "Due to train traffic, we are stopped," I feel panic rise.

I've never liked feeling trapped. Dr. Greer says it must stem from the hospital stay, but I've privately thought it might be another side effect of being a twin. I love my sister and would never want her to go away, but it's true the connection can be claustrophobic at times. Even though things are peaceful, things have been going so well with Curt that I've found myself wishing she would leave. Not forever, but I do think she should get her own place. I just never have the heart to tell her, and in the past, it's always been up to Dr. Greer and Dad and Mom. That's why she doesn't trust them.

The train jolts, and I realize I've been absentmindedly touching my scar. Dropping my hand, I say a silent thank you to God or the Universe or the subway conductor and force my mind back to Curt.

As we approach the next stop, a text comes through:

Alexa, please call me back. I love you.

Shit. Dad's called several times in the last couple of weeks, but the honest truth is I just forget to call him back. I keep my phone in my hand as I make my way up to the street. Then another notification dings.

Reminder: Dr. Greer 7 p.m.

Damn. I was so caught up in Curt's business plan that I completely forgot about my weekly appointment. It's only six thirty, thankfully, so I hail a cab and head back uptown.

In the cab, I decide to call Dad, hoping the driver won't think it's rude.

"Alexa!"

"Hi, Dad! I'm sorry I haven't called you back. I've been slammed with work."

"I know, but, Alexa, you have to be better about at least checking in."

"I know. I'm really sorry."

"Even just a text, okay?"

"Yes, of course. How are you?"

His voice grows warmer at that. "Same old. How are you?"

"I'm good! Work is going really well."

"That's wonderful. Are you on your way to Weinstein?"

"Yes, Dad, I'm in the cab now. Don't worry."

"Impossible! It's my job to worry."

I roll my eyes. "I know, but trust me. Things are really going well."

"That's great. And how's living on your own?"

I pause and will the words not to come out, but they persist.

"Well, I do have some news. My boyfriend's staying with me until he gets his own place."

"What?" He practically shouts it, his voice going up several octaves.

"Dad, I'm an adult. Remember?"

I can hear him rustling around in the background. He must have stood up, and now he's pacing.

"Oh, Alexa. I know . . . but what does Dr. Greer say?"

I stare out the window. We're passing through Union Square now.

"He knows and he's supportive," I say flatly.

"Really?"

"Yes."

"Has he met . . . have you heard from—?"

I cut him off before he can finish. "No. I told you, we don't talk."

"Oh, okay."

"I'm almost to Weinstein, so I'm going to run in," I say, even though we have at least twenty more minutes to go, given the rush-hour traffic.

"Okay. Please remember to check in, Alexa. Maybe I'll come for a visit and meet this young man."

"I'd like that," I say, and I mean it, even though with Beth I know it can't happen. I'm going to have to figure out a way to get her out, without destroying her. "Love you, Dad."

"Love you too, Alexa."

I hang up and ride in silence for the rest of the time. I couldn't bear any further probing, especially when I'm due for another hour of probing in my session with Dr. Greer. I notice that my hands are sweating, and my left eyelid has some sort of nervous tic. Did I remember to take my medicine? There's just been so much going on it's been hard to keep track. I make a note to myself to be better about that.

27

BETH

I linger outside of Dr. Greer's door and strain to listen to their faint voices. I'm about to give up when I hear Alexa's voice rise a bit.

She's upset.

"Is there a rule about how long you should date someone before you move in?"

"Of course not. But given your history, I'd recommend you take things extra slow."

"Well, you've always told me I don't have to take every recommendation. Because they're just recommendations."

"That's true."

"People get married after a few days and it lasts fifty-plus years." She's desperate for Dr. Greer's approval. I can hear it in her voice.

"That is also true. But as we have also discussed, everyone is different. What works—"

"I fucking know! 'What works for some doesn't work for others.'" She pauses and then finishes. "Sorry. I'm so sick of feeling like I'm sick."

"It's not like you to cuss," Dr. Greer notes in a gentle voice. "Why do you feel sick?"

"Because I'm always here because of what happened."

"With Beth."

That fucker. Why is he bringing me up? I fight the urge to barge through the door and defend my sister. But that will only make things infinitely worse. I made that mistake once before. Alexa didn't speak to me for almost three months.

"Yeah. I mean, no. I just mean all of it. My whole life I've been made to feel different, and I'm finally feeling normal, and I just want everyone to support me."

"Do you not feel supported, Alexa?"

"You know what I mean."

"You'd like for me to approve of your decision to move in with Curt?"

"Yes. And Dad."

"It would be irresponsible for me to support a decision that I perceive as potentially harmful to your well-being."

"Got it."

"Has Curt met Beth?"

I listen intently but I hear nothing. Are they whispering? Did I miss something? I press my ear against the door and plug my other with my finger. Silence.

"Not ready to talk about Beth?"

"I don't see how my sister is relevant to my relationship. I live alone now. I've grown up. Do you make all of your patients talk about their siblings?"

"Only when that relationship is the catalyst for every single traumatic event in their life."

I've always hated Dr. Greer but never more than in this moment. He's never been bold or aggressive—it's more his variety of manipulation that turns me off. He's coaxed Alexa to make judgments about me in the past, but this is the first time I've been present to hear him blame me for Alexa's life-moments-gone-wrong. Is he fucking crazy? Maybe he needs a damn therapist. Alexa is the one who caused all the trauma—she's the one to blame. I let that go for a long time, but that's the truth.

I've heard enough. But as I turn to leave, I hear her.

"It's not Beth's fault. I've told you that for years."

I love my sister. This is why I forgave her. Since that night when we were nine, she's proven her loyalty to me. And so I've done the same in return.

Time to get out of here before I lose my control and confront Dr. Greer. I bolt down the checkerboard halls and emerge from the glass doors onto the city streets, but then I find myself at a loss for where to go. I don't know how long I've been pacing outside the center when I see Alexa come out.

"What are you doing here?" She grabs me and pulls me around the corner of the building.

"I—"

"Come on, Beth. Jesus."

"I'm sorry. I just wanted to make sure Curt wasn't lying about working here still."

"What?" she shouts, then swivels her head to see if anyone is watching our exchange before softening her tone. "Why would he lie?"

"I don't know."

"Look, you don't have to trust him, but you have to trust me."

"Fair."

"Well?"

She surprises me with this question.

"Well *what?*" I ask.

"Is he lying?"

"Nope, he's not on the schedule, just as he says."

I watch her proud smile grow. "Duh. Let's catch a cab."

She takes my hand and hails a cab like Carrie in *Sex and the City*. It wouldn't surprise me if she knew how to do that whistle thing with her fingers too. My sister really has adapted quite well to this new, adult life. I feel a pang of sadness. Or maybe it's jealousy. I've never wanted independence and freedom as she has, but I must admit, she looks happy.

I can smell the curry as we near the door to her apartment.

"He's cooking Indian tonight," Alexa says. "He texted me earlier."

"Have you had Indian?" I ask.

"I don't know."

"It smells . . . strong," I tell her.

"Keep an open mind. Free food, Beth."

"Yeah, because he isn't living here for free or anything."

She jabs me and opens the door. "Hellooooo," she sings. "Smells awesome!"

"Hey!" he calls from the kitchen.

We poke our heads through the kitchen doorway. There must be seventeen pots and pans. Things are boiling and steaming and baking. There are sounds and smells and sights.

"What is it?" I ask.

"An Indian feast!" he shouts. "Who's hungry?"

He shuffles a few lids and pots, then turns and grabs Alexa. The moment he smacks his lips on hers, I decide to head to the bedroom. I don't know why it makes me so uncomfortable; I just feel awkward during their PDA shows. They don't even notice I've left. I turn my attention to something even more intimate. The diary. I wonder if she's destroyed it as she promised.

One by one, I open the boxes, searching their contents for the little book of our secrets. I can't find it. I check the dresser, closet, and nightstand. Nothing. I drop to the floor and search under the bed. I clamber back up and run my hands under the mattress.

Nothing.

I walk to the other side and do the same thing. I start at the foot of the bed and feel nothing until I hit something cold and hard near the headboard.

I kneel down and lift the mattress and look at the object. A handgun. It looks like Dad's old one. But it can't be his—that was taken by the police. The memory of my mother's death washes over me. The way her head rested on the table, the bright crimson blood staining the electric bill. But why does *Alexa* have a gun?

Dropping the mattress with a thump, I sit back and ruminate on this question. As I do, an even scarier question emerges. Is it even Alexa's?

I sit, paralyzed.

"What are you doing?" Alexa asks.

I whip around to see her standing in the corner. I didn't even hear her come in.

"What the fuck are *you* doing?" I say, going to the head of the bed and propping up the mattress so she can see my discovery clearly. I say nothing, watching for her response.

"Oh," she says calmly.

"Is it yours?"

"Yeah. Who else would it belong to?"

"Oh, I don't know, your boyfriend?" I whisper-shout.

"*No*, it's Dad's. I took it from his case. He has so many he'll never notice."

"Why?" I beg.

"This is New York. I don't know what could happen."

"You've had this the whole time?"

"Yeah. It's 2021. I'm not about to be a sitting duck with all the psychos out there."

I'm surprised and oddly proud. But mostly I'm relieved. The world spun into what most refer to as a "dumpster fire" beginning in 2020, with crime, riots, and criminal activity skyrocketing in every major city. Even those who swore they'd never own a gun found themselves sneaking to local shops in case a civil war broke out.

"How did you find it?" she suddenly questions.

Lost in my memories of the pandemic and its wreckage, I didn't anticipate the obvious follow-up question she'd likely ask.

"I was looking for the diary. Did you destroy it?"

"Oh. No, not yet, but I'll do it tomorrow when Curt goes to the gym."

"Where is it?"

"I hid it. Duh."

There's a knock on the door. "Dinner's ready!"

Alexa starts to head to the living room but stops when I call out for her to wait.

"You'll do it tomorrow. Swear?"

"Swear!"

In the kitchen, Curt is carrying plates so loaded that our little apartment meal could be mistaken for a Thanksgiving feast.

"Hope you're hungry," he sing-songs.

"Hope it's good!" I mimic. Alexa swats at my arm.

"I think you'll like it," he assures us as he sets down the plates on the counter.

I poke my fork at something green. I think it's chicken.

"It's curry," he says. "Have you never had curry?"

"I haven't," Alexa says.

"Never," I add.

I bring the green-covered meat to my mouth and prepare myself for a horrible taste, but to my surprise, it's spicy and the flavor is good. No, it's great. I spear another with some rice and proceed to devour the dish. I may not trust him completely, but at this point I can no longer make a case for not trusting his cooking.

"Not bad," I tell him, and he gives me one of his wolfish, too-big smiles. I eat enough to fully knock myself out, and decide that dishes can wait and a nap on the couch is in order.

28

ALEXA

That night, I manage to drag myself off the couch and into the kitchen. Work must have really killed me this week, because I can only vaguely remember eating the dinner that Curt so painstakingly prepared. But I feel much better now as I start to wake up. I reach for the bottle of Dawn dish soap and refill the scrubber brush, longing for the dishwasher at home. I'd always heard that New Yorkers don't cook because most people don't have dishwashers, garbage disposals, or, in my case, an adequate kitchen. But somehow Curt manages to produce these phenomenal meals. Taking care of the dishes is the least I can do, since he does all of the cooking.

I make my way through the stacks, pot by pot, pan by pan, until finally the last fork is clean. I pass it to Curt to dry, but instead he takes me in his arms.

"Dessert?" he asks. The subtle raise of an eyebrow followed by his lips meeting mine clarifies his proposed *dessert*. I say nothing and kiss him back. But I remember my plan for his business and want to share the idea. It's like marketing foreplay.

"Of course! But I actually wanted to tell you about a breakthrough I had for your numbers this afternoon."

He pulls me closer. "Right now?"

"Isn't success sexy?"

"Touché."

He releases me and leans against the opposite counter like a schoolboy forced to stop playing. "Whatcha got?" he asks.

"So. I did a bunch of research and found some insider scoop about what the social platforms are looking for."

"Go on, Nancy Drew."

"I think we should drop the production value, shoot real-time daily videos of what you're cooking and eating, and post them as they are happening."

"Okay, so we just use the live features. But what about the feeds and my channel episodes?"

"No. Not the live feature. We take it back to how it began: posting photos and videos in the moment. We use the carousel feature on Instagram to post the ingredients and steps to your recipes. We do a quick edit to a static video of you cooking or eating at a new restaurant. No fancy features, just a plain cut-style editing, and upload within the hour."

He looks unconvinced. "I'm not sure how that will help me to go viral."

"Well, it's what the platforms want. They're sick of the curated content feeds and overproduced videos with a million effects. They want real."

"Interesting," he says, his gaze drifting to the wall, which means he's thinking. But I'm not sure if he's thinking good or bad things.

"Hey!" I say, waving my hand in front of his face. "Earth to Curt?"

"Yeah. I'm here," he says. "Touchdown."

"If the rumor is true that they're going to take away likes, views, downloads, and all the engagement metrics, we have to do something different. Something to make you stand out."

He smiles at that, which I think is odd, but at least he seems to be taking it all in.

"I agree," he says at last.

"Cool! I'm going to pitch Christine Monday, and hopefully we can start right away." I'm relieved that he's as excited about my idea as I am. "Maybe this'll give me an excuse to leave the office to help shoot and film your daily habits," I add.

"Do you think it will be weird if I shoot here? Like, will they know we're together?" he questions.

"No one knows what my apartment looks like."

"True." But he doesn't look sold.

"You don't like it, do you?" I say. I've been slowly drifting toward him, but now I stop in my tracks.

"No! It's great. I just . . ."

I steel myself for his criticism. I've always been sensitive to criticism, but with Curt, I am mostly afraid to let him down.

"I've done some brainstorming myself over the last several months."

"You have?"

"Yeah. Well, I mean, I always think about ways to gain fame. Followers and views, you know?"

"Oh, of course." I'm a little embarrassed that I assumed he was just waiting for me to come up with a plan.

"Yeah, I have a pretty unique plan, actually. One I've been waiting to execute."

"What is it?"

He shakes his head. "It's a secret."

"You won't tell me?"

"Not yet. But trust me, you'll be the first to know when it's time to pull the trigger."

"Oh. Okay," I say, trying to hide my hurt feelings. It's not that he doesn't love my plan; it's that he doesn't want to tell me his—not only as his business colleague but as his girlfriend, his love. I force the pain back down, not wanting him to know how much it stings.

He takes my hands and brings me in for a hug. "Trust me, okay?"

Forcing myself to thaw, I return his warm embrace, enjoying his breath on the crook of my neck. Then his lips softly kiss the same spot before gently biting. A rush pulses through my body, and I forget everything.

"Dessert?" he murmurs, and I nod, letting him lead me to the bedroom.

As we pass Beth, I turn to her and say goodnight, but she has her headphones in and is watching something apparently enthralling on the open computer propped up on the coffee table. She raises a hand but never looks up.

29

ALEXA

We must make love six times that night. The next morning, as I roll over, I pray that Beth didn't hear anything.

Curt is still sleeping. I inch closer to his body, wrapping my arm around his side and nuzzling my face into the spot between his shoulder blades. I breathe in his smell, a combination of sweat and the lingering scent of curry. I feel the stiffening of his muscles as he rouses and starts to stretch.

"Good morning," he rasps, then rolls onto his back.

"Morning."

I adjust my own body to wriggle into my favorite crook between his torso and arm and delight in the warmth of his body and the sound of his beating heart. It's slow and steady. His chest rises and falls with my head on it as we lie lazily in the morning sun.

"You ready for another workout?" he asks, breaking the silence.

I respond by rolling on top of him and leaning in for a kiss.

He chuckles. "I meant the gym, but I think we have time for this warm-up too."

We make love quickly and quietly before finally emerging from the tangled sheets and dressing. Curt always goes to the gym on Saturday mornings. He goes a little later on Sundays, after he makes us brunch.

I'm not much for the gym. After the incident, everyone treated my injuries as if they were some kind of permanent disability. It got me out of gym class, sure, but sometimes I envy the girls who trot around in sports bras and leggings. I've gone with Curt a couple of times, but I feel rather out of place. Curt tells me no one cares how I look and to just enjoy the endorphin rush.

"Feel like coming with me today?" he asks.

"Sure."

The truth is I don't, but I've found that at least the gyms are pretty empty on early Saturday mornings. New Yorkers really only have one meal on the weekends—brunch—and it spans from eleven in the morning to midnight. The earlier hours are spent sleeping off Friday night.

We get dressed and leave my bedroom. The couch is empty— Beth miraculously out again.

"I'm gonna run down and grab us coffees," Curt says.

"Cool. I'm just gonna wash my face and brush my hair. I'll meet you at the corner bodega in a couple minutes," I reply.

I hear him leave and decide I should probably tend to my female duties. Men have it so easy. But maybe, just maybe, I'll lie down for a second first. I set my timer for five minutes of precious sleep, knowing it will take Curt at least thirty minutes to be back with coffee. And having an empty couch to snooze on is a rarity these days, so I may as well take full advantage.

30

BETH

I wake up feeling like shit. They were fucking all night. And this morning.

Thankfully, they're both gone when I come out of the bathroom. I make a mental note to get some damn earplugs.

But not right now. Right now, I need to search Alexa's room. Something's bothering me about what she said last night. *I hid it.* I've never not found something Lex has hidden. We are twins. We are inside each other's brains. It's nearly impossible to keep things hidden from each other. *I hid it.* If she hid it, I will find it.

I tear into the boxes again, knowing from past experience that I should have at least a few hours before they return.

When I find nothing, it dawns on me that maybe she hid it somewhere else in the apartment. That would be smart, actually. No one hides important things in plain sight. Unfortunately, the bathroom yields nothing, and the kitchen only bears the remnants of last night's Indian feast. By the time I finish combing through the living room, I'm growing desperate. Where the fuck is it? My instincts lead me back to the bedroom. I move slowly through the room and all of its nooks and crannies before finally giving up.

Collapsing on the bed, I let my head drop into my hands. What if she gave it to Dr. Greer? No, she would never do that. What if she hid it at work? Couldn't someone find it? Jesus, that would ruin her career. But maybe she has one of those locked drawers for important files? Is that still a thing? I've never been to her office. I drag myself up and am taking one last look under the bed when I hear the front door close loudly. I must have been so wrapped up in my thoughts I didn't hear it unlock.

Scrambling to get to a standing position, my face no doubt red, I turn to see Curt in the doorway holding two coffee cups.

"What are you doing?" he asks, setting the cups down on the dresser. "I got your coffee."

"I was just looking for something," I tell him, willing him to leave. How long have I been searching? Maybe they decided to skip the gym after all. He doesn't respond but instead moves his messenger bag around from his backside to his front and digs something out. Then my heart stops. He pulls the diary from his bag and places it on the dresser.

"Don't worry. Your secret is safe with me," he says.

"You took it? How much did you read?"

"Don't worry," he assures me. "I don't care, Alexa."

"I'm not Alexa. What the fuck. Why did you take it?" I try to stand, but panic makes me too dizzy. I slump back down.

"I told you, I love you and I don't judge either of you."

I can't speak. He starts back on his shtick about how he doesn't care and we all have issues—but if that were true, he certainly has done a lot of work to figure out what issues not to care about. I quickly try to discern a plan. This is what we've feared, and yet I have no idea what to do.

"Just tell me everything you know," I demand.

"I read it all. Cover to cover. Over and over."

I feel sick.

"It's really interesting, honestly. It could be a book or a movie or something. Or a television show."

"Well, it's our fucking life," I snap without thinking, my hands running over the bed covers. "Not a TV show."

"So, you guys were born conjoined?" he asks.

What happens next can only be described as animal instinct. Fight or flight—and my nervous system only fights.

As he starts to retell our horrible story, I run my hand under the mattress and pull out the gun. Understanding crosses his face just before the bullet pierces his abdomen. I didn't see Mom's face when the bullet hit, so I'm not sure if his expression is a universal one everyone has in the instant before they die. But as he stumbles back and the blood begins to flow, he does something that's shocking even to me. He smiles, and I swear I see him laugh. It lasts only a moment before he turns angry.

"I knew you would fuck this up. You moron," he gasps as he reaches into his bag. "Where's my camera?"

I fire two more bullets into his torso. His body releases the oxygen that is left and more blood.

He is dead.

The first thing I do is grab the diary off the dresser and put it under the mattress. Then I think back to all the episodes of *Law & Order* I've watched and try to stage the scene. I didn't expect this, so his gunshot wounds definitely don't appear to be self-inflicted. Fuck. Careful not to disturb the blood spatter or the body, I try to piece together a puzzle of how he could have done this to himself.

Then it hits me. Alexa's words: "I'm not going to be a sitting duck with all the psychos out here."

This was a break-in. I start to mess up the room and look for valuables to take when suddenly my eyes are drawn back to the body.

I look at his light green eyes, now glassy.

And I start to scream.

31

DR. GREER

I cannot say I was surprised when I received the call this morning. I was sad, disappointed—but not surprised. I've worked with Alexa since she was young, but I've long known she's never fully trusted me.

The truth is, I wanted to believe that we had a real breakthrough about a year and a half ago when she came into the office and told me she was ready to let Beth go. It was what I had been hoping for ever since she first came to see me, but up until then, Alexa had always defended her sister fiercely. I thought letting go of her sister meant that she'd transfer her trust to me.

It stayed that way for over a year. Until she moved to the city. I understand now that I shouldn't have supported it.

After our appointment yesterday, I took Alexa's files home, which means it's easy to gather them up on my way to the police station. The entire way, I mull over my interactions with Alexa and try to pinpoint the moment Beth came back. Did she come to see me?

When the cab stops outside the station, I pay the meter, collect my briefcase, and practice a breathing technique for stress as I make my way inside. I've had many ill patients, some of whom have sadly taken their own lives. But none have ever been accused of homicide. I think back to the initial call from Mrs. Martin; I was nervous to take the case. But the fear in her voice left me no choice.

I'm greeted by two officers who introduce themselves as Briggs and Morton. They thank me for coming so quickly and lead me down a narrow hallway to a small room. When they offer me coffee or water, I decline both. I've never been brought into the station before. With my suicide patients, they often request our records and notes, but they never bring me in.

"Thank you again for coming down, Dr. Greer," Officer Morton says once we're seated. "As we mentioned, this is concerning a patient of yours, Alexa Martin."

"It's no problem," I tell them, setting my case on the table. "I'm honestly upset that I wasn't able to prevent this."

"Well, some people can't be helped," Morton responds.

"I disagree. In fact, I still believe Alexa can be."

They exchange a look before Officer Briggs speaks.

"Why don't we leave that as an issue for later. Let's start with what you can tell us about Alexa. So far, she's been belligerent."

"I'm not surprised," I tell them, remembering some of her—or their—outbursts.

"We spoke with her father, who gave us the bullet points. He's on his way," Morton tells me. His word choice is terrible, but it's my understanding that there isn't enough training for officers, so I let it go.

"So you're aware that she first went into treatment shortly after the death of her sister, Beth?" I ask.

"Yes," Briggs confirms, and they share another odd look.

"That's the odd thing. She keeps saying Beth killed the guy," Morton says curtly.

I take a deep breath. They probably won't be prepared for the information I am about to share, but ultimately, it's not their decision on her sentencing. All I can do is explain the scientific facts.

"Right. I'm not sure if you're aware of the circumstances surrounding her sister's death, but the trauma of the event has had a rare but not impossible effect on Alexa," I begin, searching their faces for comprehension.

"Yeah, so, after her death, she started displaying erratic and dangerous behavior," Morton tells me. "That's my understanding?"

I shake my head. "Are you familiar with DID, Officers?"

"No," they say in unison.

"Multiple personality disorder?" I clarify.

"Yeah, of course," Briggs says as Morton nods in agreement.

"I'll skip the backstory, but we now refer to multiple personality disorder as dissociative identity disorder. It's the same symptoms, but our research has grown enough that it became time to reclassify."

They watch me silently. Then it's Morton who speaks first.

"So you're saying Alexa has a split personality?" he asks.

"Yes. But it's a rare case because most patients have several completely new personalities and Alexa only has one. And that is Beth."

"Her dead sister?" Morton states with unparalleled frankness.

"Correct."

"She has an alternate personality that is her dead sister? How is that possible?" he continues.

"As I mentioned, it's rare. There are only three other documented cases in the world where a DID patient identifies one of their multiples as a deceased relative."

Morton sits back in his chair and whistles. "What the fuck, man."

Morton is testing my patience with his lack of empathy.

"Alexa came into my care and was very open about Beth. I've even spent time with Beth. But shortly after their mother's suicide, that openness stopped. Beth never came to me again."

"Why would she suddenly change?" Briggs asks.

"Every case is different. We know only a tiny fraction of the brain. There's much left to discover."

"Jesus. And she was nine when this all started?" Briggs asks.

"Yes. I believe it was the trauma of killing her sister that created this rare manifestation. As I mentioned, DID is not uncommon, and we believe it is brought on by trauma."

"She *killed* the sister?" Morton asks.

"Correct. Did Mr. Martin not make that clear on the phone?"

"No. He just said the sister died," Briggs says.

"She was nine. How did she kill her? And why don't I have a record on this?" Morton questions.

"There is a death record, of course, in Connecticut," I tell them. "But they were nine, and the parents obviously didn't press charges, so there is no criminal record for Alexa."

"How did she kill her?" Morton asks again.

After what feels like hours of explaining, they finally bring me to see her. I don't see the belligerent attitude they profess, but she is confused. I spend what feels like another day trying to explain the very thing we've tiptoed around all these years: She's mentally ill and needs intensive treatment, likely for the rest of her life. When I finally emerge from the cavernous concrete building into the fresh air, I feel as if I've failed her.

I shake my head as I hail a cab and try to silence the voices in my own head, the ones that say, *You can't help this one.*

As a professional, I've let a lot of people down. But this situation is new. They put us through countless trainings meant to instruct us on how not to blame ourselves. But how can I not? If I could have cracked the code or figured out a new way, then maybe I could have saved that man's life. And hers.

Starting up my breathing technique, I close my eyes and lean back against the seat of the cab. But the image of the officers' faces when I told them how Beth died flashes in front of me like the signs on the Las Vegas Strip. I sure hope they don't make this any worse than it already is.

My phone rings and I answer.

"Dr. Greer. It's Paul Martin."

"Paul, how are you holding up? Is there anything I can do?" I ask.

"Are they going to put her in jail?" I can hear the sadness and fear in his crackling voice. The truth is, Carrie was always the one whom I worked with most, while Paul just trusted me to take care of Alexa, feeling ill-prepared to help.

"I recommended a facility over jail," I tell him.

"Oh god, I hope they do that, Dr. Greer."

"Paul, I did recommend that the time in the facility be indefinite," I say.

He's silent at that.

"It's safer for her there, and who knows? Maybe there will be a breakthrough in the field that will help."

"I hope so," he says softly.

"I'm sorry, Paul. I really am."

"Thanks."

"Please call me anytime. I told the officers I'm happy to testify and provide all my findings and notes."

"Take care of her, Dr. Greer."

"Of course, but—"

He's already hung up.

32

ALEXA

I listen as Briggs runs through the script again. My answers are the same—we've gone through this so much that I'm on autopilot.

The next time he starts up, I find it hard to keep my attention from drifting to the cold green walls. That's when I remember the other building that had green walls. Maybe it's why I've always hated green walls.

It was only weeks after my last surgery that my parents finally told me why they seemed so sad even though I was recovering well. They told me Beth had died. No, they said I killed her—took a knife and tried to cut us apart. Things were blurry, but I remembered hiding the knife on my far side that night, the side not attached to Beth, and waiting until we went to sleep. I'd only wanted a little independence, and it wasn't supposed to hurt her—I thought we could just separate and be like everyone else I saw. Maybe she'd even sleep through it, I told myself.

But immediately after the knife pierced our skin, Beth started screaming. I tried to hurry as she fought me. The last thing I remember is Mom coming in the room and the horror on her face.

The next time I opened my eyes, I was in the hospital bed. Alone.

"I have some good news for you, sweetie," the doctor said one morning. He was the one I liked—when he caught one of the nurses sneaking me an extra pudding, he just gave us a wink before carrying on. "You're ready to go home."

"Can Beth go home?" I immediately asked.

Mom and Dad looked at each other, then to the doctor. Instead of addressing my question, he began to list all the fun things I wouldn't be able to do for a while. Run, play, go to school, eat anything fun. At least I'd be home, though.

"Thank you," Dad said as the doctor left.

"Alexa, we're going to run home to get you fresh clothes and to get everything ready. Then we'll be back to take you home. Okay?" Mom said.

"Can we get pizza?" I asked.

"No," Mom said. "You heard the doctor—strict diet until you're healed."

I touched my side to feel the stiff staples and pokey stitches. "But they closed me. Aren't I healed?" I asked Mom.

"No. You have a little while until you're all healed."

Even though that made me grumpy, they both gave me a kiss on the forehead before leaving. I pressed the call button, and my favorite nurse, Maria, poked her head through the door. Her smile was always so big. Ever since she told me about her two daughters, I sometimes wished she was my mom.

"What does my favorite patient need?" she asked with her usual grin.

"Can I watch TV till my mom and dad come back?"

"Of course, Miss Alexa. What do you want to watch?" she asked and turned on the TV. It was still on the cartoon channel. Tiny yellow Pikachu poked out from behind Professor Oak's leg.

"This!" I shouted, and she laughed.

"Okay, Miss Alexa. You just rest until we're ready to let you go home, okay?"

"Okay."

I was watching cartoons when I saw the first flash out of the corner of my eye. I thought maybe Maria had come back with extra pudding—or maybe even something better since it was my last day—but it wasn't her. It was better.

"Boo!" Beth shouted, springing up beside the bed.

"Beth! Where have you been?" I asked.

"Just wandering around, scaring people," she said with a smirk, but she was lying again. She was in here the other day when I screamed at my parents that she wasn't dead, but they just told me to stop, and then Mom started crying. They sent in another doctor afterward, and he asked me so many questions, all about Beth. I still didn't understand why they didn't just ask *her*.

"Beth, why can't they see you?"

She didn't say anything. She just moved her hospital gown to the side. I gasped. Her side, the one that used to be attached to me, was a gaping, bloody hole. No one had sewn it up for her. When I looked at her face, I realized her skin had turned a grayish color.

"Pretty gross, huh?" she asked, looking down at the wound.

"Why is yours like that?" I asked.

"Don't know."

I smiled. But then I felt really bad.

"I did that to you," I said. "I'm sorry. Does it hurt?"

"No. Nothing hurts. It's pretty cool. Plus, it's not that bad here. I keep taking that nurse's phone and hiding it. She's going nuts!" Beth laughed.

"Maria?" I asked.

"Yep."

"Don't do that—she's nice."

"Oh, *relax*. It's just for fun."

She waved her little hands and signaled for me to scoot over. Then she jumped up on the bed and lay by me, just as we had every night since we were little.

"Look. You can't tell anyone when I come see you, okay?" she told me.

"Why?"

"Because they won't believe you. They're going to think you're crazy and send you off to a scary place."

"How do you know?"

"I just do. We have to keep this a secret."

"Okay."

We watched the cartoon on the TV. After a little while, Mom and Dad came back. I sat up in a panic, eyes flying to Beth, but strangely, they didn't seem to see her.

"Time for me to go," she said.

When she got up, she walked right by Dad, even brushing his arm with her hand. Why were they ignoring her?

"Dad, why is Beth being so strange? Can you tell her to stop? She's scaring me."

At that, Beth spun on her heel to glare at me. Dad was too busy comforting Mom, who was sobbing again, to notice.

"I told you," she said. "They can't see me. You cannot tell anyone that I still visit you."

Afraid to say anything aloud, I just nodded.

She flashed her wound, the one I created, before finally leaving the room. It was her voice that I heard last, saying the thing that's haunted me ever since: "You owe me, sister."

33

ALEXA

Briggs has left me alone in the room again. I stare at the walls and wait for him to return. I hear the door creak, and I'm surprised to see both officers, a man in a suit, and Dr. Greer.

"Hello, Alexa. How are you holding up?" Dr. Greer says.

I can't find words, so I nod slightly.

"Again, I'm so sorry for your loss," he adds with his signature compassion and professionalism. He always knows the right thing to say, even when it's not what I want to hear. I shouldn't have let Curt move in with us—I understand that now. Beth was too unstable.

"Thank you," I tell him.

Morton and the suited man shoot a judgmental look at Briggs. Briggs shrugs before speaking.

"Ms. Martin, as you know, this is an unusual circumstance. So, per Dr. Greer's recommendation, we have decided to move you to an inpatient facility as we wait for the trial."

Another facility. My face must fall, because Dr. Greer speaks immediately.

"Alexa, it will be far better than waiting in jail," he says. "Plus, I'll be able to check in twice a week and work closely with the team to ensure you begin treatment and get any help you want while you're there."

His careful wording doesn't escape me: "any help I *want*" as opposed to the obvious, "what I *need*."

I thank him and the officers and allow them to escort me through a different exit. This one leads to a garage, where I am ushered into a van. I prepare myself for the presumably long drive alone in the backseat. But then Dr. Greer slides in with an officer I haven't met yet.

"I wouldn't let you go alone. Your father is meeting us there," he tells me with a gentle hand on my shoulder.

I force a smile, but I feel the tears bubbling up.

My dream for a normal life is over.

34

DR. GREER

Psychiatric Unit Upstate

I'm driving down the dark highway when my phone rings. I've spent the day with Alexa upstate, and to say my nerves are shot would be an understatement. But the thought of potential updates or news forces me to hit the button to accept the unknown number on my dashboard. "Hello?" I say.

"Dr. Greer, this is Officer Briggs," the voice informs me.

"Officer. Hi. What can I help you with?"

"Look, there's no great way to say this," he begins, "so I'm just going to spit it out."

I know this voice. I know this call. I steel my nerves and begin my breathing technique and wait for him to finish.

"We've been unable to get in touch with Mr. Martin since Saturday, so we had a trooper head to his Connecticut home," he drags on.

"Okay," I respond.

"They found him dead. Self-inflicted gunshot wound to the

head." He blurts it out with the care of Bigfoot. They're all this way—it's a side effect of the job.

"You're sure it was suicide?" I ask, well aware that they're sure.

"Positive. He left a note."

"What did it say?" I ask.

Briggs clears his throat and reads. "'I'm so sorry. I thought she was gone. I thought Alexa was better. I can't handle this anymore.'"

"Have you told the facility yet?" I ask. I can't help but picture Paul hunched over, the way they found his wife just a few years ago. And poor Alexa, losing the last tie to a once normal life.

"No. We wanted to see if you thought it was okay to tell her." He pauses. "In her, uh, state. You know?"

"I'm about an hour from the facility. I'll turn back and tell her."

"Are you sure?" Briggs asks.

"It's the least I can do," I tell him. "I know she killed a man, but she's sick, not evil. I know that much. She deserves someone she knows delivering that sort of news."

"Okay," he says, and we hang up.

I take the next exit and head back to the facility. I'm exhausted and haven't slept in over twenty-four hours, but the thought of this news coming from a stranger pumps my adrenaline enough to keep me awake.

35

ALEXA

It's been almost a day since I got here, and Dad still hasn't shown up yet. Dr. Greer stayed until only an hour ago, getting me settled in and talking with all of the staff while I went through the torture known as intake, where nurses ask me a million questions. This time, though, I'm a little relieved, because they don't ask me about Curt. Or Beth. Just about me and my life.

I miss Curt. But I don't miss Beth.

I'm in a room by myself. Many patients have roommates, but they've decided to keep me alone, and close to the nursing station. It's not lost on me that my desire for independence is what led me here.

We aren't allowed TV or phones, so I spend most of my time staring blankly at a journal Dr. Greer left. I don't want to write, but I know I won't be able to sleep. It's not that I'm afraid of my dreams—it's that I'm afraid of the moment where I wake up again and realize my reality.

I hear a knock at the door and tell the person to come in. But I'm surprised when I see the guest.

"Dr. Greer? I thought you left."

"I did, but I turned back. I got a call from the officers."

I wait, hoping and praying it may be some good news.

"Your father has passed away, Alexa," he says. The sadness in his eyes keeps me from experiencing it all on my own.

"How?" I ask.

"Remember how we talked about death a few times?" he asks.

I nod.

"It's not the manner in which someone passes that gives us the freedom to move on. It's our acceptance of their passing," he repeats. He's said this to me many times.

I nod and realize I am not even crying yet. I must be too exhausted or shocked. Or maybe nothing shocks me after the last two days.

"Let's just focus on the fact that he's gone, first," he says. "Then we can work through the details."

"Okay."

"How do you feel?" he asks.

"I'm numb. I'm scared. I'm alone."

"You wanted to be alone often, but I imagine this is nowhere near what you had in mind," he states.

"I wanted moments alone. To live alone. Not to lose every single person that ever meant anything to me." I feel the tears rise as I hear the reality of my words.

"May I hug you?" he asks.

We have never hugged. In all our time together, we have never touched more than a handshake or a pat on the arm.

"Sure." I grant permission. He moves to hug me, and I try to keep the tears back, but his warm energy sends them flying out of me like fireworks from cannons, bursting onto his shoulder.

He holds me as my sob turns to dry tears. I finally pull away and see that he, too, has the familiar streaks down his cheeks. I never thought about what it must be like for Dr. Greer to work with all these people. I bet he loses a lot of people too.

"I'm sorry, Alexa. I am," he says, maintaining composure despite the tears.

"I know."

"I wanted to help."

"I know. You did."

He nods and forces a smile.

"I'll let you rest. Will you be all right?" he asks.

"I don't know?"

He nods again.

"I'll tell the staff, if you'd like."

"Thank you," I say. He stands and turns to open the door of my small room.

"Call me anytime. I'll see you in a couple of days," he says.

"Thank you, Dr. Greer."

I watch him as he opens the door and walks through.

"Dr. Greer?" I call, just as the door is almost closed behind him.

"Yes?" he says, only his head reappearing through the crack in the door.

"Was it like Mom?" I ask, already knowing the answer.

He lowers his head before nodding an affirmative yes.

"Thank you."

And he's gone. I lie back on my bed and hug my pillow and let myself drift off. There's somewhere I am supposed to be, and I'm late. Why can't I figure it out? I am stumbling through the busy streets of a big city—maybe it's New York?—looking for something I can't quite put my finger on, until I come upon my mom, my dad,

Beth, and Curt at a big pool party. That's what I was looking for! There are glass walls surrounding the party and no door in sight. I can see them but I can't get to them. They look happy. I call out to them, but they don't acknowledge me. I just watch—alone with nowhere to go—as they carry on. When I look behind me, the city is gone, and there's only a dark forest.

When I open my eyes, they sting. I realize it was a dream. The morning sunlight shines a beam of light across the room from the small rectangular window. Maybe it was a nightmare. But I take some solace in the idea of them all happy, together.

36

ALEXA

Once we get into the routine, the days here are surprisingly busy. I assumed they'd all be like my time at the police station, or immediately after intake, staring blankly at walls and water cups. But instead, they have a pretty strict and full schedule. I check the binder for today's agenda:

6 AM Yoga

7:45 AM Breakfast

8:15 AM Meds

9 AM Morning community meeting

10 AM Small group session

12:30 PM Lunch

1:30 PM Individual counseling

3:30 PM Free hour

4:30 PM EMDR

6 PM Dinner

7 PM Additional individual therapy

9 PM Bed check

It takes me a little time to adjust, but I've been sleeping better than I have in years. I'm guessing it's due to the medicine they give at lights out, but I don't complain. I've met a couple of nice patients, but our counselors warn us all to be careful. There's a lot of mental illness here.

One woman has an interesting split. She's probably in her fifties, but her multiple is only six years old. So when she flips, her voice, way of dressing, and behavior change to that of a six-year-old's. It only gets scary when her split doesn't feel like doing what the doctors say.

They video us when we split. Well, not me. I haven't split yet. Obviously, I'm not going to because no matter how many times they try to tell me Beth isn't real, I know she is. But she's definitely distant right now. I haven't even felt her near. But I know her well enough to expect her back at any time.

By the time my individual counseling session arrives, I'm excited. But when I enter the office, I'm surprised to see a third man in the room. I know Dr. Carter, my counselor here, and Dr. Greer, obviously, but the other man is new. Dr. Carter speaks first.

"Hello, Alexa," he says. "How's today going?"

"Hi. Good," I say carefully, looking to Dr. Greer for guidance. He just smiles calmly.

"Hi, I'm Tom Pearson." The stranger stands and extends his hand to me. "Your lawyer," he adds.

Oh. We've spoken on the phone, but we haven't met in person yet.

"Nice to meet you," I say. "I didn't know you were coming today."

"Neither did we," Dr. Greer adds.

"Yeah, sorry for dropping in, but they had some cases dismissed and one unplanned confession, so they've actually bumped up your trial to Monday."

"This Monday?" I ask.

"Yes."

"Isn't that too soon?" I question.

"It's soon, yes, but we feel prepared. I've spent most of the day with Dr. Greer and Dr. Carter, going over your progress and diagnosis." Tom's sitting now, pulling files from his stuffed and very shiny briefcase. "I think you have a really good shot at avoiding jail time."

"Well, yes. But, Alexa, it's important you know that the DA is still pushing for a life sentence," Dr. Greer adds with his trademark cool.

My heart stops. "Life sentence?"

"That's the recommendation for murder in the second degree," Tom states.

I can't find words.

"But we have a great case, so let's just use our time today and until then to prepare," he adds.

I look at Dr. Greer, who nods in agreement.

And so that's what we do. We spend this and the evening session preparing, combing over the details of my time in the facility so far and the progress the doctors have seen. We go over Beth and how I haven't seen her since that day in the apartment. This part is crucial. The doctors and Tom inform me that this will be our new normal until the trial. As we wrap up the last session, I ask Tom one more question.

"How long will the trial last?"

"It depends, but we'll most likely have a sentence by the weekend."

37

ALEXA

The drive to the city for court is long. Dr. Greer said he would meet us at the courthouse. As we pull up, I see he's already there, with Tom.

"How was the trip?" Tom asks as I open the door.

"Quick," I lie.

"I boxed up your things," Dr. Greer says. "Do you need me to arrange a storage unit?"

"Um, can I bring them upstate?" I ask. But the expression on Dr. Greer's face and the way Tom looks at him reminds me why I'm here.

"Actually, a storage facility would be easier. Thank you," I comply.

He nods, and I hear the voice inside my head remind me: *You may not be going back upstate.*

As we go inside, the men follow behind me the way camp counselors do so they don't lose a wandering child. The courthouse is a huge, expansive mass of concrete and marble. It's beautiful—the way the two large staircases meet in the middle reminds me more of a castle or European cathedral than a government building. I look around at the ornate details on the walls. For a moment I forget what this building means to my future. Of course, the metal detectors and airport-security-style entry process are harsh reminders.

As we pass different people, I wonder if they're here for reasons similar to mine. A set of large wooden double doors bursts open, and a petite woman with medium-long auburn hair lets out large sobs. An equally small man bursts through the same doors moments later and chases after her. Through the closing doors, I see it's a standard courtroom, several rows of seats. Then I see what must have caused the woman such suffering. A young man, probably eighteen, is handcuffed and being led by officers through a door to the right of the judge. I swallow hard and look away.

"I've arranged for us to have this room until they're ready," Tom says, and I turn to find him holding a door open.

"Shall we go through the plan again?" he asks once we're all settled.

"I think I'm good," I tell him.

"Do you want to practice the questions?"

"No, I know what happened. I know what to say."

"Do you feel comfortable?" Dr. Greer chimes in.

"As comfortable as I can be, considering I'm on trial for murder," I say with unintended sarcasm.

"Very well then," Tom says. "Dr. Greer, will you join me in the hall for a moment?"

"Why can't you talk in here?" I ask.

"We need to discuss . . ." He pauses, clearly unsure how to deliver his message.

"Beth?" I guess.

"I warned Tom that speaking too much about Beth, Curt, or anyone else you've lost could be a trigger," Dr. Greer informs me.

"Oh. I see."

"We don't want the trial to interfere with the major strides you've been making upstate," he clarifies.

"I get it. It's just that I prepared myself to hear a lot of painful things during the trial, so what's one more conversation in here?"

"Why don't we just step out and let you have a moment alone before the chaos begins?" Dr. Greer offers.

"Okay." I smile at him.

Once they step outside, I stare at the wooden walls. The paneling looks like something our forefathers stood in front of for portraits. It's old. The whole building is so old. I wonder how many people have had their freedom or even their lives taken here. I know many of them probably deserved it. But what about the ones who didn't? The ones where the jury got it wrong? I feel my pulse in my head, and I can't shake the thought. *What if they get it wrong for me?*

A short while later, Tom pops his head through the door.

"They're almost ready. Ten minutes," he tells me before disappearing back through the door.

Ten minutes. I know that as soon as we are in the courtroom, anything can happen. Including the worst. Unlike most other times in my life, I will the seconds to pass as slowly as possible. I breathe deeply, trying to still my nerves, but the fear courses through me.

The door opens again.

"It's time," Tom says.

38

ALEXA

The courtroom is small. There are only five rows of seats on either side of a small aisle, and the seats are not nearly filled—only about a dozen people have come to see my fate decided. The prosecution is composed of two men and one woman. Our side is empty.

I follow Tom to the table after giving Dr. Greer a hug. We do this often now, and it's really my only form of human contact at the moment. It wasn't long ago that my main human contact was Curt. An image of the two of us in bed flashes across my brain before disappearing. I can't even enjoy the memories, because I still miss him so much. I breathe deeply as Dr. Greer slides into the first row of seats just behind our table.

It smells musty in here. My eyes go to the two windows framed by thick burgundy drapes—I bet they've never been opened. I watch as an older woman sits at a small, isolated desk just to the side of the judge's chair. The court reporter, I guess.

The jury seats are empty. So is the judge's.

Tom tells me to sit, so I do. We wait but don't speak until the jury is brought in. I try not to stare, but I'm curious as to who will be deciding my fate. It really is a diverse group. Having never been called to jury duty, I wonder how they were selected.

"All rise," says the bailiff.

Everyone in the room stands as the judge enters. She's a woman in her fifties with tight curls.

"Court is now in session. Judge Grace presiding. Please be seated."

Everyone sits. This whole time, I've felt eyes on me, but it's her eyes that scare me the most. While it's the jury who will decide my guilt, she'll decide my sentence. I feel as if I may pass out. I brace myself for the blackout, but it doesn't come.

I listen as the judge speaks, her voice at odds with her soothing name.

"Good morning, ladies and gentlemen. Calling the case of People of the State of New York versus Alexa Martin." Her eyes fall on me as she says my name. "Are both sides ready?" she asks, looking from me to the DA.

He stands. "Ready for the People, Your Honor."

He's a big man. Not tall, exactly, but more like a sturdy square of a person. He has a clean-shaven face with dark black hair, thinning at his crown. He also appears to be sweating. As he sits, he pats his forehead with a white handkerchief. He can't be nervous—I'm the one who should be nervous.

"Ready for the defense, Your Honor," Tom tells Judge Grace.

"Will the clerk please swear in the jury?" she directs.

"Jury, please stand and raise your right hands." When the men and women do as directed, he continues. "Do you swear that you will fairly try the case before this court and that you will return a true verdict according to the evidence and the instructions of the court, so help you God? Say 'I do.'"

As the members of the jury say their "I do's," I think about how long it will be until we take the "so help you God" part out. I read an article recently about how it's illegal to require someone to say the Pledge of Allegiance since it mentions "God," yet it's God who's going to punish these jurors if they don't return a true verdict? The hypocrisy and lack of proven accountability send a tremor of fear through my body. I force the epiphany out of my head and say a prayer anyway, hoping that if God exists, he will forgive me for my lack of correspondence. *And my actions.*

"You may be seated," the clerk says.

The DA stands and begins what I imagine is his opening statement. "Your Honor, ladies and gentlemen of the jury, the defendant has been charged with murder in the second degree. The evidence will show that Curt Kempton was shot to death by the defendant, in her apartment on the morning of August seventeenth. The defendant's fingerprints were on the murder weapon, and she was found crying over the victim. Additionally, we have evidence that the defendant has a history of mental illness that was never properly treated. The evidence I present will prove to you that the defendant is guilty as charged," he states coolly, despite the sweating.

Once he takes his seat, Tom stands.

"Your Honor and ladies and gentlemen of the jury," he starts, sounding just as cold as the DA, and I realize there must be some kind of universal script for lawyers. "Under the law, my client is presumed innocent until proven guilty. During this trial, you will hear evidence that my client is guilty. You will hear evidence that my client has suffered from mental illness. However, you will also learn the truth: that Alexa Martin was not of sound mind or even in her own body at the time of Curt Kempton's murder. She would never want to harm Curt and is in fact mourning the loss of her lover. Therefore, I assure you that my client, Alexa Martin, while in sound mind at this moment, is not guilty. I understand this is a unique case, so I ask that you please pay close attention to the scientific and medical facts both sides present."

For the first time, the weight of the situation, my situation, hits me. My defense is that I have a mental illness. My fate rests on the notion that I am certifiably insane and that Beth is my sickness. The doctors at the facility and Dr. Greer have told me this, explained this to me, but hearing it as my only defense still feels like a punch to my stomach because it's impossible. My only defense is impossible, and it feels like I'm the only one who knows it.

"The prosecution may call its first witness," Judge Grace states.

"The People call the defendant, Alexa Martin," the DA says.

My heart picks up speed as I turn to Tom.

"We've gone through this," he says softly. "Just tell the truth. And if you feel . . . off, tell them you feel sick."

I nod and stand. If I feel Beth coming, I am supposed to feign illness—as if I have that much control.

The bailiff guides me to the witness stand, where the clerk swears me in. "Raise your right hand."

So I do.

"Do you promise that the testimony you shall give in the case before this court shall be the truth, the whole truth, and nothing but the truth, so help you God?" he asks.

"I do," I tell him while wondering again if God can or will help me either way.

"Please state your first and last name," he directs.

"Alexa Martin."

"You may be seated."

"Please spell your last name for the record," the woman behind the tiny typewriter-ish machine says.

"M-A-R-T-I-N," I spell out; however, I'm certain there's no question since my name is all over every document in this room.

The DA makes his way from behind the desk, and I try to calm my nerves through deep breathing. Tom told me they generally start with simple questions to warm up.

"Is it true, Ms. Martin, that you killed your sister, Beth?" he asks flatly.

Jesus. That was not a warm-up question. I freeze.

"Objection. What does this have to do with Curt Kempton's murder?" Tom asks.

"Overruled," Judge Grace quickly says. "Answer the question, Ms. Martin."

"Yes," I say. "But it was an accident."

"Can you tell the jury how?" he asks.

"I . . . I didn't mean to. I was young, and we were conjoined, and I didn't mean to," I say before breaking out in loud sobs.

A low murmur of chatter breaks out in the courtroom, and I feel sick. I actually feel very sick. I turn to the judge.

"I think I'm going to be sick, Your Honor. I just need a moment," I plead as the bile rises in my throat. "Or a trash can."

"Bailiff, take Ms. Martin to the restroom. She's going to be sick," she says.

I stand to meet the bailiff, but I feel weak, as if I may faint again. But this time everything does go black, and I'm alone in the comfort of darkness.

39

DR. GREER

I feared that this would happen. Stress is a proven trigger, and the DA led with the hardest question. Alexa is a strong young woman, but we, as humans, are not designed to handle this much.

They won't allow me to see her while she's being checked out by a physician, so I stay seated in the front row and wait for news from Tom. Most of the audience has stayed put as well. Some people have shuffled in and out, but it's relatively calm. A few minutes later, Tom appears from a side door with the DA. He makes his way to the desk, in front of me.

"Is she okay?" I ask.

"Yes. Just stressed and shaken up by his line of questioning," he tells me.

"What do we do now?" I ask.

"We just spoke with the judge, who's warned Mark to ease up on the questioning given her mental illness."

"Ease up?"

"Well, honestly, he's got to do his job and ask the relevant questions, but we need her to be able to answer," he explains. "We both need her to answer. We can't keep having her faint."

"Okay. But are we stopping for today?" I ask.

"No, they're bringing her back out. And . . ."

"And what?" I ask.

"And we hope for the best."

He says it like an underdog in a fight with no hope for a win. My heart sinks, and I sit back in my seat.

The bailiff reappears with Alexa. Judge Grace is just behind. Everyone retakes their seats and the court resumes, with Alexa on the stand.

"Okay, Ms. Martin, we're glad you're feeling better," the DA tells Alexa, and she stares at him without so much as blinking. "Let's start with something else. How did you meet Curt Kempton?" he asks.

"He was dating my sister," she states.

"He was dating your sister?" he asks her.

"Yep. I still don't get it. I guess they worked together. That's how they met."

"Don't you mean *you* worked with him?" he asks.

The man clearly hasn't caught on.

"Nope. I never worked. But Alexa was fucking hell-bent on being an independent career woman," she says and rolls her eyes.

A gasp and murmur rumble through the court, and the judge smacks her gavel several times while yelling for order.

"Ms. Martin, can you please state your name for the court reporter once more?" she asks her.

"Beth Martin," she responds confidently, and more gasps and chatter fill the room.

My Lord, she's flipped during her own murder trial. I reach

for my notepad and quickly jot down what I remember. Alexa was being questioned about killing Beth, felt sick, fainted, then reappeared *as* Beth. Fascinating.

The pounding of the gavel and Judge Grace's deep voice shock me from my notes.

"Ms. Martin, do you know why you're here?" the judge asks.

"Because I killed Curt?" she says with the same confidence and intonation as when she stated her name.

"You killed Curt Kempton, Ms. Martin?" she asks. The DA is standing with his mouth agape, sweat running down his face.

"Yep. I thought you knew that," she says.

"And why did you kill him, Ms. Martin?" the judge asks.

"Because he was going to hurt Alexa," she tells the judge.

"How?"

"He was going to expose her—or us, I guess," she says.

"And what is there to expose?" the judge asks.

"I think you know."

"Can you tell us, for the record?" she asks.

I watch, forcing myself to stay seated. I try to make eye contact, but Beth keeps her eyes steadily fixed on Judge Grace.

"Will it help my sister, Your Honor?" Beth says.

"It may," the judge says honestly.

"I take over her body," she says flatly.

"Why?" the judge asks.

"To protect her. To stay alive. Because it's fun. I don't know. I just do," she explains.

"I see." The judge turns to the DA. "Do you have anything else for the witness?" she asks him.

He takes a long pause before finally responding. "No."

"I have something else to say," Beth says. She's still facing the judge, an impossible mix of reverence and defiance on her face. She grips the railing before her, her knuckles white.

Judge Grace and the rest of the courtroom fall silent, all eyes on Beth. "Go on then," the judge orders.

"You all know Curt wanted this, right? To make him famous?" Beth states.

There's no response, until finally it's Judge Grace who asks, "Curt wanted to be famous? Yes, we know that much."

"No, he wanted to be killed. On camera. He wanted his death to make him famous, and he was planning on using Alexa to do it," Beth continues.

"What do you mean, Ms. Martin?" Judge Grace asks.

"I found his plan on his computer. Tell me you've looked at his computer?"

Chatter begins among the people of the courtroom.

"Order. Order!" Judge Grace shouts with several beats of her gavel.

The DA looks stunned, as does Tom. Surely this can't be true. There's no way. Tom and the DA approach the judge and converse for several minutes. I watch as Beth sits picking at her nails as if she hasn't just dropped a potential bomb into the courtroom.

"We will adjourn for the day. Court will resume at nine tomorrow morning," Judge Grace announces with one final smack of the gavel.

40

DR. GREER

The courtroom is buzzing, and I cannot believe what I've just witnessed. In all my years of practice, I've never seen someone flip like that. I've never seen Alexa flip like that. I need to get to my files. I need to go over everything and see what patterns I may have missed. This could be huge for the field.

But then it hits me. Alexa. Where is Alexa? If Beth is in her body, when will she be back? I see the tripod and video set up in the far corner of the room.

"Tom! Tom!" I shout over the now very loud courtroom. Just as when a teacher leaves a classroom unattended, so goes an unattended courtroom.

"What the fuck was that?" he asks.

"I need the video of today," I tell him, ignoring his question.

"Why?" he asks.

"Just get it for me. Alexa needs to see that. She needs to see what happened today," I tell him.

"Why?" he protests again.

"She doesn't know she's insane, Tom. She has to see it. Alexa is rational, but she has to see it with her own eyes. She has to see that Beth isn't alive."

I watch the comprehension unfold through his expressions, then he turns quickly and calls for the bailiff. He must know that Alexa's understanding of her own mental illness could be his way to a win.

I pace and watch, waiting for him to reappear from the judge's chamber. The door opens less than three minutes later, and Tom emerges with the bailiff. That can't be good news. I watch as they walk across the courtroom and over to the cameraman. The bailiff shows him a piece of paper, and the cameraman pulls the SD card from the camera and hands it over. Tom turns and flashes a thumbs-up before following the bailiff back to the door leading to the judge's chamber.

I wait, this time for much longer, until finally Tom reappears, this time alone. He hurries over to me and hands me a USB drive.

"What's this?" I ask.

"The tape," he says with annoyance.

"Oh. I thought—"

"They're not going to let us take the only video from the trial, so they had to burn a copy. But I've been warned that we are only allowed to show it to Alexa. And don't make copies or anything. Or sell it for any reason."

"Tom. I'm aware of how the law works," I assure him. "This is just to try to finally break through to Alexa."

"Right. So, are you going now?" he asks.

"Yes, but I've got to be sure it's her," I tell him.

"Do you want me to come too?" he asks, and I can see his desire for a hall pass.

"No. It's best I talk with her alone. I'm not sure how she'll feel about this." That part is true. I have no idea how she will react, but I know for certain that she must know. "Plus, don't you need to look into this accusation against Curt?" I add.

"You think there's weight there?" he questions.

"I don't know, but what have we got to lose?"

He nods, and I leave to see Alexa.

41

ALEXA

The clank of my cell's lock opening startles me. I turn from the small desk in the corner of the cell to see a guard.

"You have a visitor," he says.

"I do?"

He gestures toward the door, ignoring my question.

We walk side by side, his hand firmly holding my right arm as we wind our way past the visitor room. Before I can ask where we are going, we stop and he opens a small room. I see Dr. Greer seated at the table, but it isn't until he stands to greet me that I notice the laptop in front of him.

"Dr. Greer, why are you here?" I ask.

"I need to show you something."

I can tell by the look on his face that he doesn't come bearing good news.

"What is it?" I ask.

"Have a seat, and I'll fill you in."

I sit and watch as he loads a USB drive into the computer. He taps a couple of keys and clicks before seeming satisfied and turning his attention back to me.

"Alexa, we haven't really talked much about my initial thoughts regarding Beth."

I feel myself flinch at the mention of her name.

"Do you remember when we first started working together, that first time I met Beth?" he asks.

I do. Kind of. It was a normal session by all accounts, but I blacked out halfway through, and the next thing I remember is being back home with Mom and Dad. At our next appointment, Dr. Greer mentioned Beth's visit, but I didn't want to get in trouble, so I just shut down. From then on, we did this same dance, until he finally pulled back.

"Yes," I tell him.

"Given your symptoms, I was inclined to explore the idea of multiple personalities," he reminds me.

"I remember."

I hated that thought. Beth wasn't a personality; she was there. I just never understood why everyone else didn't get it.

"I am not sure what you remember from court today, but I believe my initial instincts were correct."

"Dr. Greer, I can't do this right now. You know how I feel and what *I* believe," I tell him firmly.

"I do, but, Alexa, I think you need to watch the video recording of the trial today."

He turns the computer to face me, and I see the picture from earlier today, with me on the witness stand.

"I know what happened. I was there," I remind him.

"Alexa, your understanding of the truth is the only way you will be able to avoid prison," he argues.

I take a deep breath and watch the screen as he hits play. The DA is questioning me, but I quickly realize I don't remember these questions. Or my answers.

"He was dating your sister?" the DA asks.

"Yep. I still don't get it. I guess they worked together. That's how they met."

"Don't you mean *you* worked with him?" he asks.

"Nope. I never worked. But Alexa was fucking hell-bent on being an independent career woman."

I feel my heart race. I hit the space bar to pause the tape and look at Dr. Greer.

"What is going on?" I ask him. "That's me?"

"Yes. But . . . ," he begins.

"But that's Beth," I finish, and he nods.

"Yes. I think that when you fainted, that's when Beth came," he clarifies. "There may be other times you've blacked out, and you just don't realize it."

"But I see her," I tell him.

"Did you see her yesterday when she was on the stand?" he asks.

I rack my brain, but I can't remember anything. I was on the stand, I felt sick with the DA's horrible questions, and then I was back in my cell. I just assumed I came back here after I fainted.

"I don't think so," I finally tell him.

He closes the laptop and swings his chair around to face me. "I know this is a lot to take in. But, Alexa, as you know, we believe you have dissociative identity disorder. We have gone over this before, but do you feel any differently seeing it?" he asks, searching my face for understanding.

"How is this possible?" I ask, feeling the emotions begin to surface, first in the form of anger. "What is going on? Where is Beth?

What the fuck?" I realize I'm shouting, but it's not until I see the panic on Dr. Greer's face that I realize I've thrown my chair. A guard enters, and Dr. Greer puts up a hand to stop him.

"Alexa, it's okay. This is nothing to be ashamed of."

"I'm not ashamed! I'm confused!"

"I know. It's very confusing. So confusing," he says.

"So, Beth came to court? Why are they not arresting her? She's the one who's done all the horrible things. The cat. Our mom." My anger has turned to tears. I lean back against the wall and slowly slide down to sob into my knees.

"Alexa, I need you to hear me. To try to understand. It's the only way to keep you safe," he tells me. But I can't stop crying. As my body heaves and the tears stain my prison uniform, I feel him sit next to me and place a hand on my back.

"Beth died. She died before you even made it to the hospital that morning. She has been gone for a very long time. What you've been seeing is a trick your brain created to help you cope with the loss."

"You think I made her up?" I ask, trying to catch my breath.

"No. I don't think you made her up. I think our brains are incredible. I think your incredible brain tried to protect you from the pain you were going through. This is not your fault. This is a real thing that happens to people," he says with empathy and warmth before adding, "You're not alone."

I wipe my eyes and force myself to lift my head. "So, Beth is dead?"

"Yes. For thirteen years."

"And my mom is dead?"

"Yes."

"And my dad?"

"Yes."

"And Curt," I state, though I know Curt is dead.

"Yes," he confirms.

"Then, Dr. Greer, I'd say I'm pretty fucking alone," I say with all the energy I have left. The statement jolts him. I watch his eyes redden.

"Yes, you are alone in regard to your family. And I'm so sorry for that, Alexa." His voice shakes momentarily before he steadies it. "But what I meant was that you are not the first person to have a brain that does this to protect you. And you're not alone as you go through the rest of this trial and whatever therapy lies ahead."

I feel him stand next to me, so I force myself to look up at him. He's extended his hand. With a deep breath, I reach up and take it. He pulls me to my feet and hugs me. I let him hold me for a moment before pulling away and asking the obvious question: "Now what?"

"Get some sleep, and tomorrow we will stick with our plan and explain to the court that it wasn't your right mind that committed the crimes," he tells me.

"Will I go to jail?" I ask.

"We are waiting to see if they find anything on his computer."

"You believe her?" I snap defensively. "Plus, wouldn't they have already looked at his computer and whatever else they look at when someone commits a crime?"

"It's my understanding that they don't comb through personal effects of the victim unless there is no suspect in custody."

I huff audibly.

"We are still recommending that you go back upstate to the facility for treatment in any case," he concludes.

"Is there a . . ." I trail off, unable to ask the question since I'm still unable to fully understand my situation. He must know what I'm thinking, because he responds.

"There are many treatments that have had success. And we continue to research and push forward for more solutions every day."

The door opens, and the same guard pokes his head through the doorway.

"Everything okay?" he asks.

"Yes. We are actually wrapping up. Ms. Martin needs to get some rest now," Dr. Greer says calmly.

"Thank you, Dr. Greer," I tell him. I've been thankful several times throughout our time together, but never like this.

"It's going to be all right. Please try to get some rest."

I nod and follow the guard through the door. But as I do, a thought pulses through me like lightning.

"Dr. Greer? Will I see her again?"

"We don't know."

I turn back, dissatisfied with the answer. I'm not sure I want to see her now, but I'm equally unsure if I'm ready to never see her again.

42

ALEXA

Restless nights have always been a part of my life, but tonight, even more so. Every time I think I'm about to drift off to sleep, Beth rouses me in the form of a thought or a worry. I can't help seeing myself—or seeing *her*—on the witness stand. I can't seem to understand everything Dr. Greer told me earlier. Beth has always been here. I've seen her. Others have seen her.

Curt met her. How can it be? My mind flashes back to the video. I jolt up as the thought smacks me across the face: Did Curt know?

I'm trying to retrace every piece of my life. I'm trying to piece it together, like a giant jigsaw puzzle, but it seems impossible. Beth is dead.

"Yep. I'm dead," she tells me.

She's sitting on the other end of the cot. I flinch.

"Jesus, why are you so jumpy?" she asks, reaching out to poke me, although of course I don't feel it.

I can't speak.

"What's wrong with you?" she asks again.

"Why are you here?" I finally ask her.

"I came to check on you. This whole trial thing is nuts," she explains.

"I'm fucking insane. You're dead. I can't be talking to you."

"You're not insane!" she shouts. "Who fucking told you that?"

"Yes. I am. You're dead," I tell her sternly.

"Eh, what's alive anyway? I'm here, aren't I?" she chides.

"I don't know!" I shout.

"Shut the fuck up!" a voice yells from down the hall.

"*You* shut the fuck up!" Beth yells back.

"Stop!" I whisper-shout to her.

"Shit, you're a mess, Lex. They can't hear me anyway."

"How can I relax? If it's true . . . if what they are saying is true, then you're dead and my mind has been doing horrible things. I've done horrible things, Beth."

She sighs. "Oh, come on."

"Don't you get it? I would never have hurt him. But you take over me and do horrible things!" I hear my voice rise.

"I'm not kidding, bitch, shut up!" the voice down the hall yells.

Then it hits me.

"Mom. Curt. Susan?" I say aloud, though she already knows. "I killed them. Not you, because you're dead! How insane is that? I'm crazy."

"No, you're not. I'm here. I'm real."

"No. You're dead. And I'm sick of this. I'm sick of you doing this. I didn't mean to kill you, Beth. I didn't. I just wanted to be able to be alone for one minute," I tell her. "Didn't you?"

She looks at me coolly before replying, "No. I was fine waiting for the surgery."

"What if it never happened?" I ask.

"I was fine with that too," she says, her expression never changing.

"Well, I wasn't, but I didn't mean to kill you. I just wanted to be alone for once."

"You already mentioned that."

"I want to be alone now."

"No, you don't."

"Yes. I do. I want you to leave," I tell her again.

"Curt wanted this, Alexa."

"What? No, he didn't. You need to leave."

"If I leave now, I will literally never come back," she states.

I just stare at her.

"No, I'll *never* come back. No matter what," she says.

I turn and stare at her before telling her in my firmest voice, "Get out."

She stands from the bed and walks toward the door, never turning to look at me. I close my eyes tight, and when I open them, I'm in my cell completely alone.

43

ALEXA

The sound of the alarm shocks me from a deep sleep. My eyes sting and my head feels groggy, like after an evening spent with too much wine. Not that I'm an experienced drinker, but one night Curt took me to this chocolate wine bar on the corner by my apartment. I'd walked by it many times but never stopped in until we were together. We shared almost two bottles, although I think Curt's pours were slightly heavier for himself. The night was a blur, but the morning was flat-out painful.

As I go through the motions in the communal bathroom, I notice that despite the physical heaviness in my body, I feel different, almost lighter. It must be the lack of sleep. At FLLW, we'd have random work-life balance seminars, which almost all included the importance of sleep. Sleep regulates weight, emotions, hormones, thinking . . . it essentially regulates life. Sleep and water. Apparently, we need nothing else.

I finally look at my reflection as I finish brushing my teeth. My eyes are hollow, and my skin is pallid. I look for her. But for the first time ever, I only see me. The vision of my own eyes looking back at me, only me, sends a shiver through me. I think back to what she said. *Curt wanted this.* Beth was a lot of things, but something about this statement haunts me. I gather my things and walk back to my cell to change for court, ruminating on my time with Curt and anything I may have missed.

There are more people in the audience today. Is it an audience? It seems odd to me that people would want to watch a trial when they don't know anyone involved personally. But come to think of it, Curt had many people who knew him from his videos. Word must have traveled about the case. I'm mulling over why they weren't here yesterday when I see the camera being set up in the same far corner of the room. It's probably because of what happened yesterday. Because of Beth.

"All rise," the bailiff commands. And we follow the same script as the day before. I think briefly about law school and how it must be a game of memorization. Laws, scripts, cases. Tom stands, and I realize I've missed the beginning of his conversation with Judge Grace.

"Well, if there is no new evidence to submit, then let's resume," Judge Grace directs.

No new evidence. I am unsure what this news means to me. They didn't find anything on his computer because he would never do what Beth claimed. I knew it. I feel relief, even joy, knowing Curt's name has been cleared once and for all. But just as quickly as the joy washed over me, the meaning of Curt's cleared name resounds through every nerve in my body. I'll be found guilty. Or insane. Or both. I feel everything and nothing at the same time.

"Your Honor, the defense calls Dr. Robert Greer to the stand," Tom states, and the judge nods her head.

I watch as Dr. Greer makes his way forward. The clerk swears him in, the same way he swore me in the day before. With that, Dr. Greer takes a seat and shoots a closed smile to me. I nod.

"Dr. Greer, can you tell the court how long you've worked with the defendant?"

"Roughly thirteen years."

"How did the defendant come into your care?" he asks.

"Her late mother contacted the Weinstein Center. I met with her mother, and given the symptoms, we decided to bring Alexa in for an evaluation."

"What did the evaluation conclude?"

"With any form of mental illness, it can take time to give a proper diagnosis. But our initial inclination was that she was suffering some sort of post-traumatic stress from her sister's death."

The words sting.

"Can you explain her symptoms and treatment?" Tom asks.

"Well, her symptoms and treatment plan changed over the years. What specific part would you like me to explain?" Dr. Greer challenges Tom.

"Everything," Tom counters.

Dr. Greer takes a deep breath and begins telling the story of my life, starting at age nine. While he does, I force myself to think of happier thoughts: my job at FLLW, my apartment, Curt. As I continue my trip down happy memory lane, I hear Dr. Greer recount our conversation from last night.

"I have been very cautious with the diagnosis for Alexa, but last night we had a massive breakthrough. I showed her the video from yesterday's proceeding," he says as he gestures toward the camera. "And I believe she finally understands what has happened— what *is* happening—to her."

"And what do you recommend, professionally, as a sentence for the defendant?" Tom asks.

"I think she needs to be in serious treatment, not just for the disorder work but for all of the trauma and loss."

"No further questions, Your Honor," Tom says and turns back to join me at the table.

The DA is up next. He strides forward confidently.

"I won't ask you to recount your lengthy history for the jury, but can you tell the court who Alexa Martin has killed?" he asks.

Dr. Greer lowers his head before responding. "Her sister, Beth."

"And Curt Kempton?" the DA asks.

"Objection!" Tom shouts. "Speculation."

"Sustained," Judge Grace responds. "Please keep this to facts."

"Well, given the evidence we submitted yesterday, it's assumed she killed Mr. Kempton," the DA insists. "She's all but confessed, since her sister, Beth, is her, and she is Beth, as we saw yesterday."

Dr. Greer remains quiet.

"So you recommend that she be in treatment and then released? Despite the fact that she's a known threat to others and to herself and is clinically diagnosed as mentally unstable?" the DA asks.

"I'm a doctor, not a lawyer, but if the point of our legal system is to punish and rehabilitate, then I recommend the latter where it's possible, and yes, I do believe it is possible. Alexa was not in her right mind when the crime was committed."

"What about when she killed her sister?" the DA adds.

"Objection!" Tom shouts again.

"Overruled," Judge Grace shouts back.

"She was nine, a child, and not in my care. This trial is for Curt Kempton's murder, not Beth Martin's," Dr. Greer says firmly.

I listen as they talk about me as though I'm not here. As though I'm some kind of monster. But I don't know that monster. I think back to my childhood, being attached to Beth for those nine years before that one night. Why did I do it? I try to think back, but the memory has always been so hard to grasp. I close my eyes and try hard to rattle any second of a memory loose. Then I hear her.

I did it.

I open my eyes and see the courtroom hasn't stopped at this statement, and I watch as I hear it again.

I did it.

I'm not saying these words; it's Beth. She's here.

I said I'm not coming back, and I won't. But I did it. I wanted you to stop fucking complaining about being conjoined. I couldn't take it, always having to agree on where to go, what to do. I was ready for that independence too, she tells me, and then I see it.

And I feel it. I clutch my side as I see that night clearly. I was asleep when the tearing of my flesh woke me. I choked on my own scream before ripping the knife from Beth. Mom and Dad came racing into the room, but Beth was already unconscious, and I was holding the knife. The next thing I remember is waking up in the hospital and everyone telling me I was responsible for the "incident."

I'm too afraid to speak back to her, but I wait for her to say something else. But Tom's movement startles me. He and the DA are walking to Judge Grace, and Dr. Greer is stepping down from the witness stand. What did I miss?

Tom walks back shortly after speaking with the judge, who has banged her gavel and called for a recess. "She wants to speak with us during the break. I'm not sure what's going on—I haven't had this happen before, to be honest. The whole case is new for me, actually," he says.

I see the bailiff reaching for me, and I stand to join him. He walks me back to my cell to wait. I lie back on the bed and say the words that have been bursting inside of me ever since Beth spoke.

"Why did you let me think I did it?"

Silence. I wait. But she never responds. I file the question with so many others I have that remain unanswered, and drift off to sleep. I only wake when I hear the door unlocking again.

I'm not sure if it was a dream or if it was her. But we were outside on the beach, holding hands. And in the sand, I saw the words spell it out. *Curt wanted this.* Then I watched as she dropped my hand and walked out into the crashing waves. She walked slowly, deliberately, each step submerging more of her body. I didn't move or try to stop her. When the crown of her head disappeared, I watched the ribbons of her brown hair slip under the dark ocean water, erasing any evidence of her.

I replay the scene over and over as the guard leads me back to the courtroom. Once he releases his hand from my arm, I sit and finally say, "Goodbye."

He shoots me an odd look.

I wasn't speaking to him.

44

ALEXA

This time, I rise before the bailiff can tell us to do it. Judge Grace makes her way back to her seat at the center front wall of the courtroom. Once she permits, we all sit back down. Tom shuffles folders into his briefcase before settling into his seat.

"What happened during the break?" I whisper.

"They came to a decision," he tells me.

"Already?" I say with palpable fear.

"Yes. As I warned you, it's a pretty easy decision for the jury, given the evidence," he says, and my heart sinks. "But it's the judge's sentencing that will decide your fate."

"I think I'm going to be sick," I tell him.

"Now?" he asks. "You have to wait."

I nod, realizing that I won't empty my insides on the courtroom floor and it's just the terror coursing through me. Odd that they feel the same.

"Will the jury foreperson please stand?" Judge Grace asks.

An older man stands. His skin is tanned to the color of a

baseball glove, while his scalp clings to what hair remains. He must be in his sixties.

"Has the jury reached a unanimous verdict?" the judge asks.

"Yes."

His voice shocks me. I was thinking he would have one of those raspy cowboy voices from the movies, but his is light, high-pitched even, like a young boy.

The clerk reaches out a hand to the tanned man and collects a piece of paper. I presume that paper will decide my fate. The clerk walks quickly back to the judge and hands her the paper. She looks it over before handing it back to the clerk.

Closing my eyes, I wait to hear the words we've expected from the beginning.

"The jury finds the defendant guilty."

I turn to Tom, trying to fight the tears welling up inside. I knew this was coming, but now it's real.

"It's okay. We knew this would happen. You have to keep it together until we find out the sentencing."

The tears pour down my face, but I don't make a sound. A choir of murmurs fills the court room. Judge Grace is slamming the gavel over and over.

Finally, the crowd quiets, and the judge finds my eyes with hers.

"Ms. Martin, I'm confident in the decision of the jury. There has been absolutely no evidence to refute the fact that you killed Curt Kempton."

I wrap my arms around my middle, clutching my scar in one hand. I bite my lip to keep from sobbing as I wait for her to continue.

"I've sentenced many to life or more for committing the exact crime you've just been convicted of." She pauses, letting the silence build like an avalanche ready to break free and crush me. "However, this case is unlike any I've ruled on, given the nature of your condition. I do believe that you loved Curt. I do believe that you were not in your right mind when you shot him. And I do believe that you are remorseful for your actions," she says, continuing to hold my gaze.

I nod over and over as she speaks these truths, my truths.

"And Ms. Martin, I do believe that you didn't mean to hurt your sister." Her face has thawed, like a mother scolding a child she doesn't wish to punish but must. "No matter what mindset you are in, however, you've proven that you are capable of taking a human life, and for that reason, it's my responsibility to keep the public safe. And to keep you safe."

She clasps her hands together and rests them in front of her before dealing the final blow.

"For those reasons, you are sentenced to Rickman Psychiatric Facility indefinitely. You will be monitored for your time at the facility, and you will be eligible for release only after it is determined that your condition is permanently healed and you are no longer a threat to anyone."

I'm frozen, unable to be happy but also unable to be sad. This is the best-case scenario given the situation, but I'm numb. Tom has turned to hug me, and I feel a hand that I presume to be Dr. Greer's on my shoulder.

"Do you understand, Ms. Martin?" the judge asks.

I nod. "Yes."

She nods and offers me a quick closed smile. "Then the jury is thanked and excused. Court is adjourned. Bailiff, please escort Ms. Martin to the transport van."

And with those orders, a blur of people move around, and I'm whisked off to the van, Tom and Dr. Greer chasing closely behind. When we reach the enclosed garage, I thank them.

"Take good care of yourself. And . . . ," Tom says, and I watch as he tries to find the words. "Get well soon."

I offer him a smile despite the awkward word choice. I'm apparently insane, not fighting the flu. Either way, I'm grateful he was able to keep me from prison.

"I'll be working with the facility to see what I can do to help," Dr. Greer says as he pulls me in for a hug. I'm still not entirely comfortable with the hugging, but I let him. I can feel the relief in his embrace. He probably beats himself up at night. All this time, I never considered how many others he's trying to fix. Guilt consumes me for all those years I took him for granted. He didn't have to keep trying.

Once he releases me, I climb into the van and watch out the window as we leave the garage. The sunlight shocks me like a sudden light in the night. I feel my eyes narrow as they try to adjust. I lean my head against the window, but I feel myself falling asleep before we even leave the city.

45

DR. GREER

Upstate New York is stunning in the spring. While the air remains crisp, it's warm enough for the highways to be lined with a green canopy. When I turn off the exit, wildflowers peek out from the bright green grass. They're not fully in bloom yet, but the last signs of winter have left.

As I wind through the back roads, I see glimpses of the Colonial-style homes not far off the highway. It always surprises me when people picture only the city when they think of New York. So much of our state is untouched and picturesque.

The parking lot is half-full, as per usual, as most visitors come on the weekends. The midweek patrons are normally other psychiatrists, psychologists, doctors, police, and government officials here to conduct follow-ups and check-ins.

I find a spot in the center of the lot and walk across to the winding pathway that leads to the reception area. The outside of the building is serene—if one ended up here by accident, he or she would be forgiven for thinking it was a particularly large bed and breakfast. I head inside, and a young woman I haven't met before greets me.

"Good morning. May I help you?" she asks.

"I don't believe we've met. I'm Dr. Robert Greer, and I am here to see a patient."

"Oh, yes, Dr. Greer—it's such an honor to meet you," she tells me, extending her arm across the counter to shake my hand with an unusual amount of energy for such a petite woman. "I'm such a fan of your book."

"Oh, yes, thank you," I say politely. In truth, I'm still not used to the attention I've received since the book. Shortly after the trial, I wrote a candid account of what it's like not to be able to help people. My colleagues strongly discouraged me from exposing the pain in therapy, but I felt as though I had to. I never spoke of specifics or mentioned names, of course, but I did share what it was like not to have the answers. Therapy is expected to cure people, and while sometimes it does, more often than not it doesn't. We're all a work in progress, some with more work to do than others.

"Do you know your way to Alexa's room?" she asks.

"I do, but I'm actually meeting her with Dr. Montgomery today."

"Oh, right! Follow me," she says as she heads down a hall.

When we arrive at the small office, the woman knocks on the door. Dr. Montgomery gave me the option to stop coming, but I can't. Alexa's lost her sister, her mother, her father, and her boyfriend, almost all while she was under my care. I can't abandon her now. But I do believe in letting the staff here guide her treatment—I'm just here to help where I can.

"Thank you. It was nice to meet you," I tell the young woman. She smiles and makes her exit back down the hall.

"Dr. Greer, great to see you," Dr. Montgomery says when I open the door. "How was the drive up?"

"It was great. It's already so beautiful up here. Living in the city, I sometimes forget what nature and spring look like," I joke, then cut straight to the point. "How's she doing?"

"She's doing well. Really. It's unclear if she's being truthful, but she says she hasn't seen Beth since the night before the sentencing."

"Wow. That's good," I tell him. "But she's done this before, for over a year one time."

"Right."

"But this time it's real."

I hear her voice before I see her. When I turn around, her face is bright with a smile.

"You look great!" I tell her as I stand. "So, tell me about these treatments."

"Dr. Montgomery can probably explain them better . . . ," she begins, and he wastes no time diving in to the details of their current treatment experiments. I listen as he recounts the EMDR, Somatic Experiencing, equine therapy, hypnotherapy, acupuncture, and so on. But it's her face that I pay the most attention to. She looks different—lighter and more alive. She was bubbly and happy when she met Curt, but not this free.

After we finish, Alexa invites me to stay for lunch, but I tell her I must get back to the city.

"More patients?" she asks.

"I'm afraid so."

She stops abruptly as we're walking through the twisting garden path that leads from the back offices to the parking lot. The tulips, gardenias, and hydrangeas aren't wild, but they're equally stunning. They flank her as if we're in a Frida Kahlo self-portrait.

"Can you help them?" she asks.

"I'm going to try," I tell her. She appears to swirl the thought around before accepting the answer. Then she starts walking again, and I follow suit.

In the parking lot, we say our goodbyes.

"Keep up the good work," I remind her.

"Thank you, Dr. Greer. I'm grateful for all of your help. Really."

At that, all I can do is nod.

As I reach my car, I open the door and flop down in the seat. Her words were kind. Too kind. I didn't help her. In fact, I've always felt that I failed her—and sadly, others. I start the car and make my way back to the road.

A light spring rain spats on my windshield, like the tears I was unable to cry all of these years. I think briefly about all of my patients, then my mind flashes to a snapshot of Curt as I've seen him in all the media since the sentencing. He wasn't my patient, but perhaps he's the one I let down the most. The trial and the case received a lot of attention in the medical field and in the media for the unique sentence. Despite how relieved I was for Alexa to be spared from prison, it was Curt that kept me filled with sorrow. The poor young man, killed by his lover with no murderer to really pay for the crime.

EPILOGUE

YouTube Headquarters
One Year Later

We're in the conference room for our weekly Monday meeting, and Phoebe is assigning tasks to my fellow interns.

"Run the weekend numbers."

"Set up the meeting for Thursday."

"Please handle the SWAG closet. I can't find a thing in there."

As she continues, I wait patiently for my assignment. I'm only a month into my summer internship, and so far, I haven't been assigned anything but mundane tasks. I haven't even been assigned a coffee run. I'd delight in the chance to leave my desk for the dreaded SWAG closet. Then I hear it.

"Rae. I have a special project I need help with. Can you stay behind a moment?"

I stay put, running through the possible project scenarios as the rest of my colleagues file out of the glass door.

"Okay, so this project is of a sensitive nature," she says, leaning across the extra-long glass table. "I'm sure you're aware of the Curt Kempton murder." It's not a question. Phoebe has never been one to pose questions.

I nod. "Of course. So sad. That crazy girl murdered him."

"Yes. Well, we're coming up on the anniversary, and we'd like to run a special tribute video on the homepage this Friday," she explains.

"Oh, yes, that would be so nice," I say, unsure of how much sympathy to show.

"I need you to go through our archives for videos and clips from him. Perhaps things he never used but that we can compile to honor his talent."

"Sure. Of course."

"Great. You know how to find his file on the shared drive?" she asks.

"Yes."

I make my way down the halls of gray cubicles to the IT department. When I see Omar's at his desk, I breathe a sigh of relief. IT never seems to be around when I need them.

"Hey, Rae. How are you settling in?" he asks with a warm smile.

"Good! I like it here," I tell him. "So, Phoebe assigned me an interesting project involving Curt Kempton's archives."

"Oh?"

"Yes! A tribute video."

"Cool. We have a decent backend that lets us go back to all of his published videos, as well as ones in the queue that he hadn't published yet." He pauses. "Do you need help accessing them?"

"Well, I know how to access the main files on the shared drive, but I haven't dug around much else on there," I admit.

"No worries. I'll show you how to get there. Follow me."

I follow Omar through the building to the "Cell." It's where all of the computer and video equipment lives, and no one is supposed to go in there unless they're in IT or Engineering. The Cell is filled with rows of black boxes with blinking lights and infinite wires. It's cold, but the buzz of the machines suggests they're warm to the touch. We pass through to a back room I never knew existed. Inside, three engineers sit at desks working on various projects that far exceed my pay grade.

"Hi, Mike," Omar says to one blond engineer. He replies with a wave.

I follow Omar to his desk, where he quickly taps a combination of keys to unlock his computer. "Come around here," he directs.

He navigates to the shared drive, and so far it's pretty familiar, but instead of accessing our team folder, he clicks on one titled *Talent* and then *Platform Backup*. I watch as he follows these digital breadcrumbs until we finally land on *Curt*. He clicks on the folder, and a long list of files shows up.

"Wow. I had no idea he had this much content," I say. "Looks like I'll have a lot to comb through."

"Eh, should be pretty easy to snag a few clips. I'll email you the path to this folder, but save it this time, huh?" he says with a smile.

"I promise. Thank you!"

I return to my desk, where I open my email and click the link Omar sent. Immediately, the folder opens on my computer, and I feel almost dizzy with the file options. I scan the list, looking for a particularly interesting recipe, perhaps, or anything unpublished. There are an overwhelming number of files, so I click on one at random. Almost instantly, Curt's familiar face pops onto the screen. He's in a kitchen I don't recognize. It's tiny. He's dressed in sweats. I check the file name and see "rehearsal_NoPub.mov." I watch the video and mark the time code of a particularly endearing part that may work for the montage.

Hours pass, and the eerie feeling that I had at first fades as I watch video after video. I'm nearing the end of the final folder, and I've only selected ten clips. I'm growing nervous that I may not have enough content to present to Phoebe.

I take a sip from my water bottle and roll my head to relieve some tension that seems to have built during the course of this project. My eyes land back on the screen and seem to fall on one particular file. In between a litany of food-pun-titled videos, I see one named "KillerContentRehearsal_PubTBD.mov." I click on it, thinking some more laid-back, almost candid rehearsal footage may be exactly what I need.

Curt appears on the screen in a white T-shirt and familiar Apple earbuds. He appears to be sitting on a bench in the park. This change of scenery reinvigorates me—everything else has been in some kind of a kitchen or studio.

"So, you guys know I love cooking, but you may not know about some of my other, more personal projects. Since we lost one of my idols, Anthony Bourdain, to suicide, I think it's important for me to open up and really connect with my followers."

He stares into the camera as he says this. I smile as I prepare myself for some more personal content. Phoebe is going to be so happy.

"I spent time at the Broughton Rehab Center in Maine a couple of years ago," he says. "And I have battled my own problems, but as an aspiring influencer, I went primarily to do research."

I lean into the screen and adjust the volume on my headphones. Then I mark the time code.

"I knew this influencer game was going to be challenging. With the algorithm changes and oversaturated market, I knew I needed to be more creative. More inventive," he says, leaning back—I can tell he's recording this on his laptop.

"Legacy has always been important to me. I am here on this

planet to create and influence, but I can't do that if I only have thirty thousand followers," he argues, and I agree. "So, I met Kyle at this facility, and he told me about how he got himself shot by officers in an attempt to commit suicide. They call it suicide by cop."

I realize this is not at all what Phoebe will want, and I move my hand to pause the video, but before I can, I hear him say, "So that gave me the idea to commit suicide."

I freeze, and the video keeps playing.

"It just kind of hit me, the way I think all great ideas hit geniuses," he boasts. "I need someone to kill me, on camera, to go viral. That would surely solidify my fame and legacy forever.

"I obviously didn't find the right person at Broughton, because, you know, well, I'm still here," he says with a chuckle. "So I started working in the kitchen at the Weinstein Center. Truth be told, I needed to hone my culinary skills, and it's chock full of psychos, so I was killing two birds with one stone.

"When I met Alexa, I knew she'd be perfect. I'd read her file," he explains. "So I hired her company to help with my engagement and marketing, but mostly, I wanted to get to her."

I'm aware that my mouth is agape, but I'm still frozen. His green eyes stare at me, as if he's telling me his dirty little secret. I can't turn away.

"So, if anyone ever finds this little video, then I will have picked the right girl," he says.

My mind swirls and races. I reach for my laptop as the video still plays.

"And you now have *killer content*. So send me viral if I haven't already."

I grab my laptop, hard drive still connected, and run down the hall to Phoebe's office.

READER'S GUIDE

1. In *Do You Follow?*, social media is critiqued in a light, humorous, and satirical way, yet is depicted as having earth-shattering consequences. Please discuss the portrayal of social media and its role in the book. Do you agree with how it is portrayed?

2. Why do you think the author chose New York City as the setting for this novel? What sort of atmosphere and effect is created by using the Big Apple as the backdrop for the story? How would *Do You Follow?* be different if placed in a small, rural town?

3. What role do the allusions to the pandemic play in the book? How would losing these mentions impact the reading of the book, in your opinion?

4. Bidonde uses Alexa's journal as a tool for creating tension in the novel. Symbolically and metaphysically, what else does the journal symbolize?

5. Is there another book or movie that is similar to Beth's and Alexa's story? Is there a fascination with twins in our culture, whether it be scientific, comical, or morbid? How does *Do You Follow?* explore themes of twindom?

6. What elements of sibling relationships does Bidonde explore in her book that are universal—regardless of whether one is a twin, or whether one has a normal or abnormal relationship with their sibling?

7. As a reader, do you have a preference for Alexa or Beth as characters? Which one do you relate to more, or have more empathy toward?

8. What was your initial reaction upon discovering that Alexa and Beth were conjoined twins and then that Beth was dead, as we encounter this information somewhat late in the story? How did you feel about this by the end of the book?

9. Once you knew Beth was not a "living" character, did you care about her any less? Did it change the stakes or the way you read the book?

10. Alexa is not of sound mind when she is charged and permitted to serve her sentence in an asylum. Do you feel that, if she were a real person, she would receive a similar sentence? Should someone like Alexa then be allowed to return to society if they ever received an all-clear on their mental health?

11. Though Alexa's therapist is a likable protagonist, he fails in saving Alexa from her fate. Is the author making a point about the effectiveness of intervention for mentally ill patients? What is your own opinion, and did the book sway or influence you at all?

12. Do you think Curt deserves any empathy? Is he the bad guy, a victim of social media and/or mental illness, or a combination of both?

13. What are your thoughts on how suicide is depicted in this book? Did the death of Alexa's father influence your opinion? Given that he has a daughter who will be directly affected by his death, do you consider it a selfish act? Do you think the author has an opinion on this topic, or is it ambiguous?

14. Do you think adolescent readers could gain anything from reading this book, or should the audience be limited to adults?

15. If there were to be a *Do You Follow? 2*, how do you envision it unfolding? Do we want to know more about Alexa's life after Beth, or is the ending a satisfying one that should remain untouched?

AUTHOR Q&A

Q: Your novel highlights the deadliness of certain social media platforms. In general, social media is critiqued in a light, humorous, and satirical way in the story, yet is depicted as having the potential for consequences as earth-shattering as Curt's suicidal demise. Can you discuss your intentions in the portrayal of social media in the book?

A: I believe that social media is not inherently bad or good. It's a tool, like other technologies we have. It's still so new to our society and we are learning its effects, both positive and negative. I wanted to keep the FLLW offices and characters bubbly and light—the way social media can be for some—and then use Curt as a contrast from the other end of the spectrum. My intention was to highlight how different social media can feel depending on the individual.

Q: What gave you the idea to use the journal as a tool for creating so much of the tension in the novel, making it the page-turner that it is? What considerations did you have in crafting the suspense your novel generates? Any tips to writers on building suspense?

A: I developed the premise line first, so I knew the basic plot line and the characters. Instead, I had to dive into their relationships and the scenarios that would create suspense while allowing the story to unfold. I knew Alexa and Beth had this secret—well, secrets—but I needed there to be something tangible threatening to expose them. I also had to take into account that most of their trauma happened at childhood, and a journal or diary that housed deep dark confessions seemed plausible for a child. In the first draft, many of the existing scenes didn't exist. I went back through several times to see where I could ramp up suspense. I think that's the best advice I can offer; first, write the story, then go back and see where you can flesh it out.

Q: Your book is set in New York City during a time when the COVID-19 pandemic is ending, but its aftereffects can still be felt. Can you share any of your own feelings on why you chose the setting you did, as well as the political climate you chose to anchor the book in? Was the pandemic instability and Alexa's instability—as well as the general instability of big-city life—an intentional pairing?

A: I chose New York simply based on my love for the city. In many books and films, New York becomes a character. I didn't want that for this book, but I felt like having Alexa move to the big city would ramp up the anxiety for her character in a subtle but consistent way. I wrote the first draft in 2019 before the pandemic. I spent most of 2020 editing, and one editor I was working with commented that this book would likely come out in a post-pandemic world. I think I'm not alone in wishing we could pretend COVID-19 didn't happen, but it felt almost irresponsible to write a book that is set post-2020 and act like the pandemic didn't happen. I also wanted the story to feel contemporary, and for the foreseeable future, we'll be navigating this new way of life, and Alexa was not exempt.

Q: Alexa and Beth are identical twins. The fascination with twins and their perceived strange abilities has always been a studied element of psychology and is culturally expressed in motion pictures and literary art. Can you speak to this, and your particular interest in twins?

A: I am fascinated with human relationships, specifically family dynamics. I don't have much experience with twins, but in developing the premise line, I wanted to use duality in a way that was unique. I read an article in which Margaret Atwood spoke of her inspiration for *The Handmaid's Tale*. She said that all of the things in the book have happened before, just not all at the same time. This was some of my inspiration to come up with something complicated, but not impossible.

Q: Do you have a preference for Alexa or Beth as characters? Which one of your creations do you relate to more, or have more empathy toward?

A: I have so much empathy for both characters and, not unlike the real world, there are things that annoy me about both and things that I relate to. They are complex characters, who are each fighting their own battle. Alexa is weaker but has a sweetness and naiveté that is endearing. She almost comes off as the underdog you're rooting for. While Beth is hardened, edgy, and bitchy, she is also loving, fiercely protective, and has a good sense of humor at times. I think readers will gravitate toward one more than the other, but I thought it was important to keep readers unsure of who to trust, rather than to make it clear from the start.

Q: How difficult was it to delay the reveal that Alexa and Beth were conjoined twins, which we discover very late in the story?

A: I knew that I wanted to keep the story fast paced, and in order to do that I needed to keep the major reveal toward the end. So, I don't feel it was hard for me to keep that secret until late in the story. I think it was harder to hint at it because it was so clear to me, but I'm hoping those hints will throw readers off until the truth is finally revealed.

Q: The character of Beth is a figment of Alexa's imagination, a result of her personality disorder, brought on by Alexa losing her twin sister when they were nine years old. Yet, Beth is a fully formed character. Can you expound on the challenges of creating a character that is not actually living, yet is a character nonetheless?

A: It was very difficult, probably the hardest part of writing this story. I wanted Beth to have a perfect set of rules, but in the process, I remembered that mental health doesn't follow any rules. So, I embraced the messiness of writing a fully formed character that was a figment of Alexa's imagination the same way I interact with mental health—with curiosity and compassion. What may not make perfect sense to one person, may be clear as day to the next. I threw out the rules and let Beth take form the way I imagined Alexa to have created her.

Q: The reader discovers truths gradually as the narrative progresses, and much of what we believe gets deconstructed as we see the contents of the journal. Through the journal, we learn that Beth is not real, and therefore did not kill Alexa and Beth's mother, Curt, or even the family cat. One reveal negates another, thereby keeping readers on their toes. What challenges presented themselves as you crafted a plot structure containing multiple levels of reveals?

A: I stand corrected, this was the hardest part. Every time I thought I had it clearly laid out in my head, I'd end up confused again. It felt like I was in a giant corn maze, trying to navigate to the finish. I finally took to writing all the major plot events on index cards, and I arranged and rearranged them many times until the path was clear. When people ask me what the book is about, I still pause. There are so many layers, which is exactly what I wanted. I wanted the reader to feel a bit unsteady, the way the characters in the book felt, but it was definitely challenging.

Q: Alexa's psychologist plays a major role in the book, and though he is a likable protagonist, there is a great deal of ambiguity surrounding the effectiveness of intervention for mentally ill patients. Can you describe your interest in this aspect of the story and/or why you chose to paint his character the way you did?

A: I am a supporter and believer in therapy. However, I think we often look for an easy fix in our culture, and what I've learned about mental health is that there may not be a perfect solution. It can be a lifelong process requiring constant work. I don't look at Dr. Greer as having failed his patients; he sees himself that way because we are all hard on ourselves. But I wanted to keep this story as real as possible, and the truth is that life can be unfair and hard. There isn't always a happy ending for every scenario or every person. That's part of the beauty of life to me, and Dr. Greer was the perfect character to show that in a loving way.

Q: How do you feel about punishment for individuals not of sound mind? Alexa is permitted to serve her sentence in an asylum. If she were a real person, should she be allowed to roam free if she were to ever receive an all-clear on her mental health?

A: I really struggled with this. As a true crime fan, it was a reach but not impossible for someone who is deemed mentally unsound to avoid jail time. I thought it was the best option for Alexa, given that we root for her and feel bad about all that she's gone through. I wanted to keep her hope for a "normal" life alive.

Q: The courtroom scene is very authentic. Many writers need to write plausible courtroom or deposition scenes. Can you tell us how you researched the best way to achieve this effect, or offer any tips to aspiring writers?

A: I watched *A Few Good Men* and *My Cousin Vinny,* hoping that my favorite courtroom movies would give me the transcript for a courtroom scene, but unfortunately, I had to conduct quite a bit more research. I read through public court documents online but found most of the help from trial law class role play documents.

Q: Did sibling relationships, either your own or those of people you know well, inspire the relationship between Alexa and Beth? In what ways?

A: I'm an only child, so I have never had that relationship, which is probably part of why it's so interesting to me. I used what I've observed through life and books I've read. I think even if you haven't been in a particular relationship, there's enough inspiration out there to be able to write about it.

Q: Was there a favorite chapter for you? Was there one that was especially difficult to write?

A: The epilogue was probably my favorite. It was one of the first chapters I wrote. I was so eager to finally let the readers know how awful Curt was. The court chapters were the most difficult because they required the largest amount of research and needed a lot of revisions.

Q: Because of the complex backstory, self-editing was most likely a must in terms of the logistics and making everything "line up." Do you have any comments on this part of the process? How were you able to deal with complicated chronology and did you do any research on this?

A: Self-editing was nearly impossible. The manuscript changed quite a bit from the first draft to publication, but this was particularly challenging given the complexity. If I changed one part, it was like pulling a thread in a sweater and unraveling the whole thing, so it took a lot of patience and help.

Q: When did you first realize you wanted to write a novel, and what motivated you to pursue this path? Did any books in particular inspire you?

A: I fell in love with reading at an early age and therefore dreamt of writing professionally. As I got older, I pursued different career paths but found writing to always be at the center of what I loved to do. I took an online course in which I learned to develop a premise line, and it was in that class that I developed this story. I knew if I could come up with a good idea, I would take a shot at writing it.

Q: Can you share a little about your writing process? For example, is there anything special that you do, such as keeping journals, writing at a scheduled time, or attending writers' groups?

A: I really want to have a routine or special hack, but the truth is I'm a binge writer. I'll sit down some days and tons of pages will come out of me, and then there are times I won't write for a month. But for this book, I stuck to a plan rather than a schedule. I perfected the premise line. Then I wrote all the major scenes on note cards and arranged and edited until it made sense. Then I wrote everything chronologically, except for the epilogue, which I did first. For the first draft, I worked with an editor whom I sent pages to bimonthly to keep me on track. This was paramount in my success of actually finishing the book, which I have been told is the hardest part.

Q: Who supported you most in your *Do You Follow?* journey, and how important do you feel that support was? Or was writing a solitary and individual act for you? Do you have advice for writers on how much (or how little) to rely on support (whether from family or beta readers) during the process?

A: Sarah, the editor I worked with for the first draft, was very supportive. Writing can be a pretty solitary career choice in its nature, so having her right alongside me was the team element I needed. I also found the premise line course to be a major part of this as well. The instructor worked with us over the weeks to make sure the premises worked, and his support was probably the reason I decided to give it a shot. So, thank you, Jeff Lyons!

Q: Are you currently working on any literary projects, and can we expect another work of fiction in the future? Alexa is a young heroine, just beginning her life, even if she has found herself in the psych ward. Could you envision writing a sequel in which Alexa has left the mental health care facility and is ready to give New York another stab?

A: This is probably the question I have been asked most by those who have read the book. I had no intention of writing the next part of Alexa's story, despite knowing that many will want to know what happened to her. I wanted to leave that part up to the reader, continuing with the ambiguity we felt throughout a lot of the book. I'll have to give it some more thought, but I don't have any plans to tell the rest of her story just yet. I am working on another project, though. It's a story about untraditional family dynamics and the effects certain choices have on the paths our lives take.

ACKNOWLEDGMENTS

When I was little, I had a white desk that was shaped to fit into the corner of my room. It looked out the window to our backyard, over a bed of "Jessica Roses" (imagine how it went when I found out that they were not, in fact, Jessica Roses but simply red roses). I'd sit at that desk and write stories of trees sugared with snow, poems about the roses, and songs, despite my complete inability to do anything musical. When I'd tire of writing, I'd read one of the many books I was lucky to have as the daughter of an elementary school teacher. It's hard to say which I love more, reading or writing, but when I step back, it's clear that my love is actually of stories—to read, to write, to tell, to hear. It took a long time to get the courage to write my first novel, and there are many people who helped to make it possible.

I took a class online called The Anatomy of a Premise Line from Stanford Continuing Ed, taught by Jeff Lyons, and it turned out to be far more than I could have imagined. I was looking to dabble in creative writing and entered the class with no idea what my premise line would be. Jeff, with your incredible guidance, I was able to develop the premise line for *Do You Follow?*. I am eternally grateful to you and your anatomy of a premise line.

I'm not sure I would have been able to complete the first draft of the manuscript if it weren't for Sarah Welch. Sarah, you held me accountable for pages and kept an open mind as we tried to work through this very complicated story. I can't thank you enough for your patience, persistence, and belief in this project.

To my team at Greenleaf—I dreamt of sitting down at some big conference table to sign a big book deal like I saw in the movies. But when it came time to publish this manuscript, I knew I needed something different. From my very first call with Kesley to David's extreme patience as I slowly worked my way through the contract, it's because of your first (and lasting) impression that I had no reservations publishing with Greenleaf.

To the editorial team, thank you for helping me cross the finish line. I knew I needed help sorting through the messy layers of Alexa and Beth, and Ava, you were a lifesaver. Your enthusiasm and understanding of these characters inspired me to polish and finally finish this manuscript. Writing this has been challenging (and a bit mind-numbing), but having someone to brainstorm and talk through ideas with was priceless. I'm not one for mushy—but I feel incredibly grateful to you for getting inside Alexa and Beth's head with me. Thank you!

To my dad and Mary, who are perhaps my harshest critics, thank you for being my first readers. I waited anxiously for your evaluation, and it's because of your support that I was able to publish this book how I wanted. That's a gift few aspiring writers have, and one I'll never forget. Thank you for your generosity and your support.

To my mom, you have been my biggest cheerleader since the day I was born. You have encouraged me to be unapologetically myself and to try anything and everything at least once. You told me I looked great when I wore Christmas sweaters in July as a kid, and you encouraged me to take the guitar lessons despite my inability to do anything musical. You are more than just my mom—you're my best friend, and I'm insanely grateful for that.

Bud, I am fully aware that you may not read this book until it's available on tape or unless I read it to you—but I want to thank you here regardless. It's really quite simple—I would not have been able to write this book without you. We share a life and, with that, responsibilities. You took on some of mine so that I could live my dream. I'll find a way to repay you, but it will not involve another puppy. I love you.

Finally, I want to thank a special group of people who shall remain anonymous. I was inspired by each one of you, in many different ways. The lessons you taught me and stories that we shared will always be some of the most important and pivotal of my life. Without our time together, I don't know where I would be or if I'd have enough clarity to write a story like this.

ABOUT THE AUTHOR

J.C. BIDONDE is a longtime reader and first-time author. She dreams of writing her next novel from an Italian villa in Tuscany with her husband, two dogs, and cat.